THE CONVERGENCE
BOOK ONE

ARMAGEDDON

G.W. MULLINS

LIGHT OF THE MOON PUBLISHING

ISBN: 978-1-958221-21-1

First Printing

This is a work of fiction. Names, characters, businesses, places, events and incidents are either the products of the author's imagination or used in a fictitious manner. Any resemblance to actual persons, living or dead, or actual events is purely coincidental.

Light Of The Moon Publishing has allowed this work to remain exactly as the author intended, verbatim, without editorial input.

Printed in the United States of America

For further information, on his writing, visit G.W. Mullins' web site at http://gwmullins.wix.com/books

For books available from G.W. Mullins in Hardback,
Paperback and eBook

Visit: https://gwmullins.wixsite.com/books

Or scan the QR Code below

Links to G.W. Mullins pages are on Linktree
https://linktr.ee/gw.mullins

What begins as a simple, bittersweet tale about a man turned into a polar bear, grandly unfolds into a rich, mythical adventure, in this best-selling book series.

Based on Hans Christian Andersen's fairy tale, author G.W. Mullins expands on this classic story creating a new mythology that takes readers into the land of snow and ice.

G.W. Mullins

Rise Of The Snow Queen
Book Series

The Polar Bear King
War Of The Witches
The Story of Gerda and Kai

Rise Of The Snow Queen Series

What begins as a simple, bittersweet tale about a man turned into a polar bear, grandly unfolds into a rich, mythical adventure in this best-selling book series.

Based on Hans Christian Andersen's fairy tale, author G.W. Mullins expands on this story creating a new mythology that takes readers into the world of snow and ice.

Long before the adventures of Gerda and Kai, this story takes readers to a remote mountain village, where winter claims lives, at the Snow Queen's command. The story goes back to the Mirror and how it cracked, sending its shards into the world to infect the innocent.

This reimagining, embarks on a much more adult tone with the mood turning rather sinister, as the Snow Queen battles to obtain the mirror. The story will capture and pull you in as Gerda and Kai make their appearances by the third book in the series.

Rise Of The Snow Queen Series

Book One: The Polar Bear King

Book Two: The War Of The Witches

Book Three: The Story Of Gerda And Kai

From The Dead Of Night
Book Series

Death is only the beginning.
Daniel walked in the land of the Dead.
Now the Dead want him back

Daniel Is Waiting

Daniel Returns

Daniel Awakens

Daniel's Fate

G.W. Mullins

From the Dead Of Night Series

Death Is Only The Beginning. Daniel walked in the land of the dead. Now the dead want him back!

Daniel Stratton died in a tragic accident. His life should have been over, but it was not. His spirit spent the next sixty years trying to communicate with the people who came to the cemetery. Then, Jen came one night to the mausoleum, seeking refuge from a life that was spinning out of control. It was there she found Daniel.

As they work to free him from the cemetery; they learn that the Light comes for all dead, Daniel is forced to enter it. Inside he sees seven Shadow People within the light, and each one marks him. Daniel knows these Shadows will come for him. Each one in the body of human who has just died. To survive, Daniel and Jen must escape the "Shadows" that are coming for them.

From the Dead Of Night Series

Book One: Daniel Is Waiting

Book Two: Daniel Returns

Book Three Daniel Awakens

Book Four: Daniel's Fate

Messages From The Other Side Series

Best-selling author G.W. Mullins shares his personal journey towards understanding death, the afterlife and communication with spirits of loved ones who have passed over. In "Messages From The Other Side Stories of the Dead, Their Communication, and Unfinished Business," Mullins tells of dealing with the grief of his mother passing and the reassurance of an after death communication that totally changed his outlook towards death and grief.

This book not only tells of Mullins' personal journey into understanding but also guides others to understand why we receive communications and the signs to look for. Mullins also explores visitation dreams and tells of his own personal experience in the area and shares the stories of others who have had similar experiences.

This book highlights the author's personal journey in an exploration for knowledge, and his understanding, without question, there is life after death.

<u>Messages From The Other Side Series</u>

Book One: Meassages From The Other Side

Book Two: Crossing Over

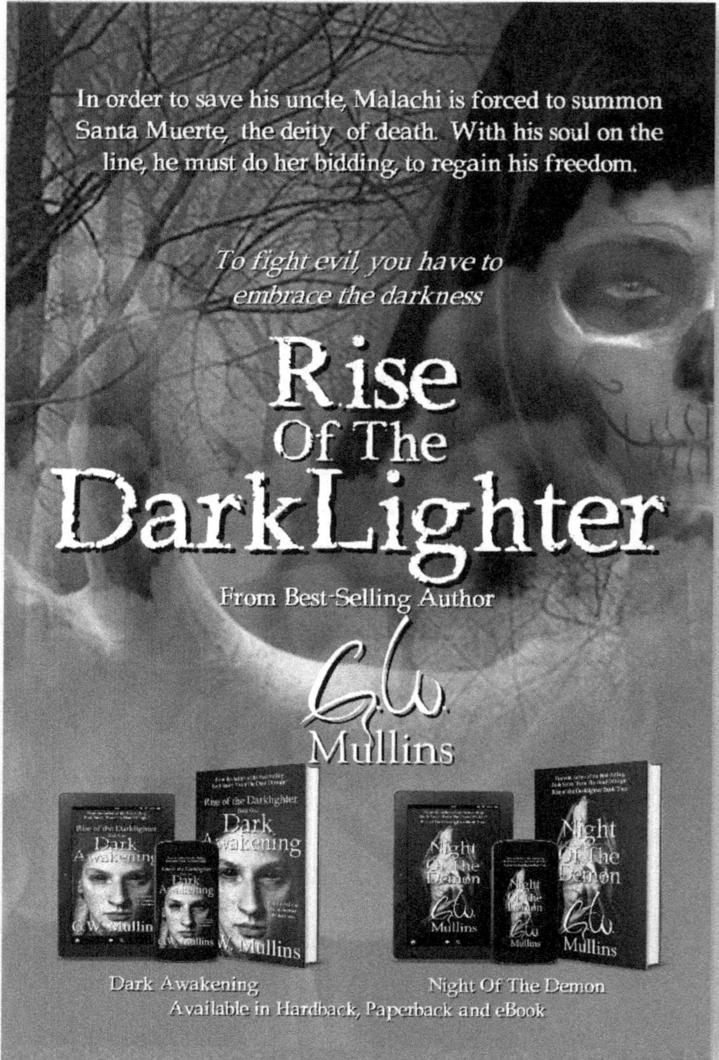
In order to save his uncle, Malachi is forced to summon
Santa Muerte, the deity of death. With his soul on the
line, he must do her bidding, to regain his freedom.

To fight evil, you have to
embrace the darkness

Rise
Of The
DarkLighter

From Best-Selling Author

G.W.
Mullins

Dark Awakening
Night Of The Demon
Available in Hardback, Paperback and eBook

Rise Of The Dark Lighter Series

Mullins returns to the familiar world he created for the "From The Dead Of Night" series, while building a new story in this universe. In the book "Daniel's Fate," Mullins left his audience with an ending that promised more. In this latest book, he delivers with a continuation of the final battle between good and evil.

In order to save his uncle, Malachi is forced to summon Santa Muerte, the deity of death. He offers a year of his life in exchange for her help. With his soul on the line, he must do her bidding, to regain his freedom.

The dead begin to rise, as Angels and Demons prepare to wage war for control of humanity. Malachi must choose a side as Armageddon begins.

"Dark Awakening" is the first of three books from "Rise Of The Dark Lighter." This new series is a continuation of his "From The Dead Of Night" books.

Rise Of The DarkLighter

Book One: Dark Awakening

Book Two: Night Of The Demon

Vengeance
A Paranormal Murder Mystery

"Mystery, Murder, Paranormal Events, and a story that leaves you guessing as the bodies stack up."
– Matthew Trent OutLoud Magazine

After the death of her father, Danni starts a new life in a seaside town in New York where she and her mother move into a strange Gothic house with a terrible history. From the moment Danni gets there, she feels she is being watched. She is sure they are not alone in the house.

As Danni learns of her new home, she is told of a past resident who fell to her death on the nearby cliffs at the same time that her teenaged daughter, Elizabeth, disappeared.

Elizabeth's spirit, appears to Danni and claims that her mother's death was a murder, not suicide and asks for Danni's help in bringing the dangerous killer to justice.

The mystery unfolds as Danni enlists the help of the hunky new friend she has made named Joe. A romance develops between them, but does Joe know more about the murder and disappearance than he is letting on? Will Danni live to solve the murder?

Dream Walker Series

They say a dream is a wish, but what they forgot to mention, nightmares are dreams too. As the city darkens and humans descend into sleep, a powerful being enters the Earth Realm. This mysterious creature, known as the Sandman, takes control of our dreams and battles for control of souls.

After a boy named Zach is taken into the other realm, he awakens to a new world filled with nightmares. He is joined by two others, Daniel and Jen, as they battle to escape the Dream World, and find their way back to reality. Beware the Sandman is coming.

"Enter The Sandman" is the first of three books from Author G.W. Mullins' "Dream Walker" book series. This new series, shares a couple of familiar faces from the Best-Selling "From The Dead Of Night" books, featuring the Best-Selling titles "Daniel Is Waiting" and "Daniel Returns."

Dream Walker Series

Book One: Enter The SandMan

Book Two: Wide Awake In Dreamland

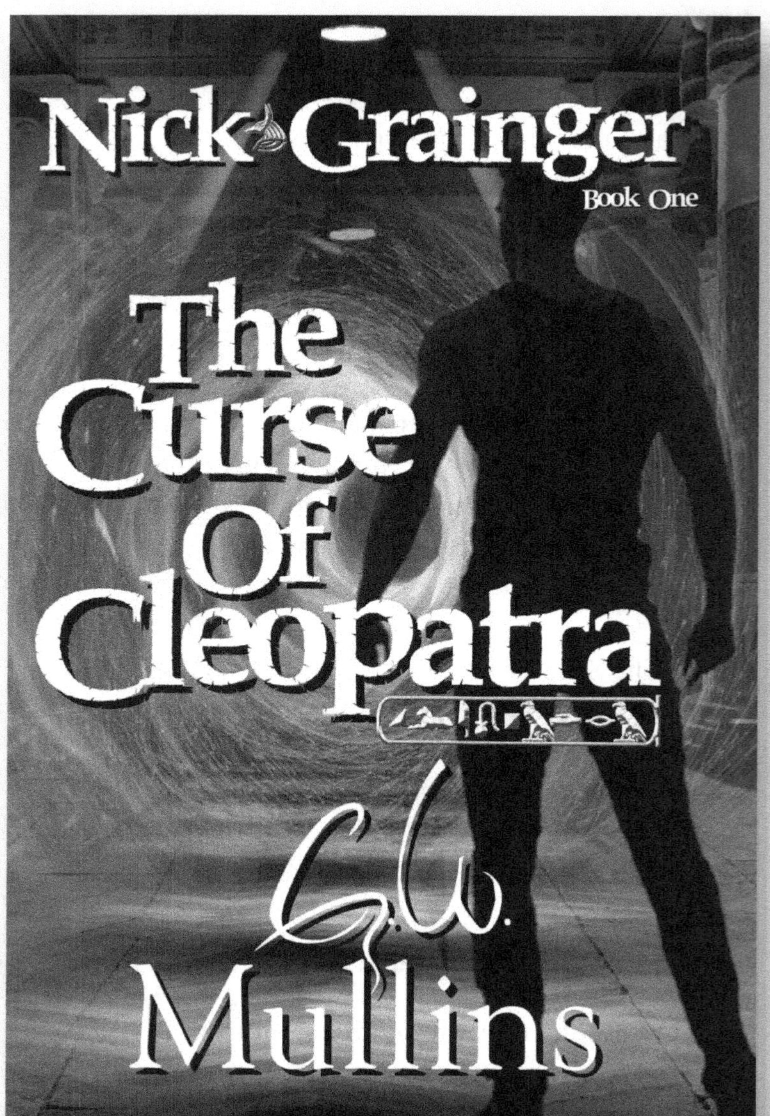
Nick Grainger
Book One
The Curse Of Cleopatra
G.W.
Mullins

Nick Grainger Series

Building on the concept that the Earth was once populated by a superior Ancient Alien race, this new book series takes the reader on an adventure through gateways to the multiverse.

Nick Grainger, a young college student working on an archaeological dig in Egypt, accidentally activates a gate to a different universe. He along with three of his companions, are thrown into the ancient alien gateway system between parallel worlds. Lost in the multiverse, they must search for a way home.

On their journey, their gate opens into strange new worlds, similar to their Earth, but in different times and in places. It is on one such Earth, they arrive in Egypt, not as it was in the days of the ancients. Now, it is a place where a technologically advanced race of gods rule.

These new gods of Egypt live through taking the bodies of human hosts. It is there, Nick must fight his ultimate battle, as he is designated to be host to the god Anubis.

"Nick Grainger The Curse Of Cleopatra" is the first of three books from Author G.W. Mullins' "Nick Grainger" book series.

FROM THE AUTHOR OF "RISE OF THE SNOW QUEEN - THE POLAR BEAR KING" AND "DANIEL IS WAITING"
THE LEGEND OF WHITE BEAR
Extended Edition
EVERYONE HAS A BEAST WITHIN THEM.
G.W. MULLINS

The Legend Of White Bear (Extended Edition)

Nita's tribe faced the coming of the bear every full moon. When it came, many would die.

To protect his daughter, the chief sent her away to live in a rip in time and space, called the void. He told her it was for her protection, but he never told her of the bear history.

One member of his tribe, was burdened with carrying the bear shapeshifter trait. For a lifetime, they would be cursed with being both human and bear until their death. Then a new child would be born to carry the trait.

While in the void, Nita discovers the true horrifying history of the white bear.

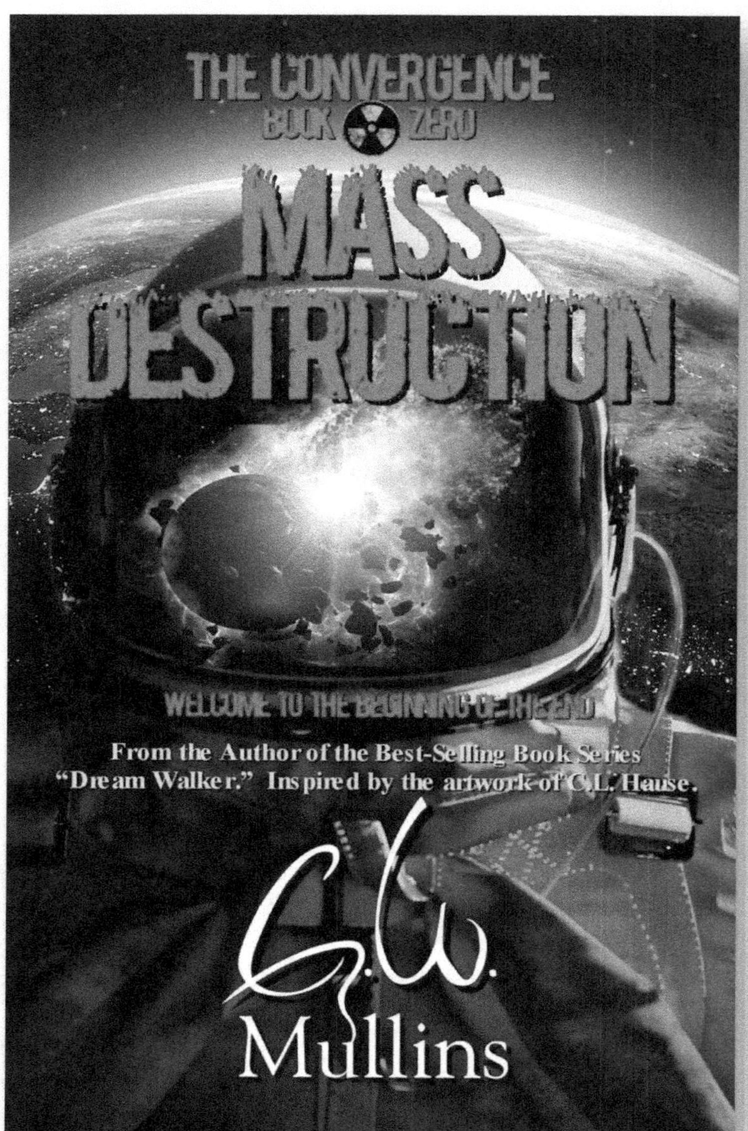
THE CONVERGENCE
BOOK ZERO
MASS
DESTRUCTION
WELCOME TO THE BEGINNING OF THE END
From the Author of the Best-Selling Book Series
"Dream Walker." Inspired by the artwork of C.L. Hause.
G.W.
Mullins

The Convergence Series

In the year 2029, the third world war will begin. After the global population is pushed to the brink of insanity from the recent pandemic, they plunge into hatred and violence. With the space race to colonize the moon, man seeks a refuge from the insanity, and the impending environmental destruction brought on by decades of pollution.

In the worldwide confusion, the inevitable happens, when a single nuclear warhead is fired by the command of an insane dictator. Nuclear retaliations are sent forward, ending in a destruction of the Earth's moon. The end of mankind as we know will begin. Human civilization is cast in ruin. A strange new world rises from the old; a world of mutation, super science, and magic. Witness the Convergence. The countdown begins now.

The Convergence Series

Book Zero: Mass Destruction

Book One: Armageddon

Other titles available from G.W. Mullins include:

Timeless - An Adult Paranormal Romance Novel

Aliens, Gods, And Other Paranormal Native American Tales

The Native American Story Book Volume 1-5-Stories Of The American Indians For Children

Walking With Spirits Volumes 1-6 Native American Myths, Legends, And Folklore

The Native American Cookbook

Star People, Sky Gods And Other Tales of The Native American Indians

More Star People, Sky Gods and Other Paranormal Tales Of The Native American Indians

Armageddon

For Clarence

"What difference does it make to the dead, the orphans and the homeless, whether the mad destruction is wrought under the name of totalitarianism or in the holy name of liberty or democracy?"

Mahatma Gandhi

"Only the dead have seen the end of war."

Plato

Armageddon

THE
CONVERGENCE
BEGINS

Armageddon

Mullins

Armageddon

(From ***The Convergence*** Book 0 ***Mass Destruction***)

The End Is Now

"Why do you look so scared, Comrade Patrick?" The Russian cosmonaut asked, as he laughed studying the other man's reflection in the glass of his console.

"I'm not scared, so much as, I don't know how to react to the experience of floating free in space. I mean, this is the real thing." He replied.

"You chose to accept the position of captain; of this space ship they are building. What do they call it now? Discovery?"

"Who knows what it is called this week. All I know is, they are putting me through every training that is known to man." Patrick said, shaking his head as he turned to look out of the space station's window.

"I would not worry, if they chose you, then they must be sure of your abilities. Besides, you may end up being one of the few who survive. Tensions are great, war is eminent. If your ship gets off the ground, you and the people living on it, may be the last people of Earth."

"Wow, thanks…that was not too much pressure to put on me."

"Calm yourself, the space walk will commence in 15 minutes. You had better get suited up."

"Pavel, can I ask you something?" Patrick said, staring into the man's face.

"Yes, what would you like to know?"

"If World War 3 does break out, would we still be friends?"

The Russian began to laugh, "What makes you think we are friends now? I am only kidding. We have known each other for some time. I do not trust very many people. You, I trust with my life. We would probably be friends no matter what."

Armageddon

Patrick turned and floated down the corridor. His stomach turned at the thought of what was before him. He doubted himself, and the role he would lead in saving mankind. If the war did not kill humanity, the state of the environment was about to.

The environmental crisis that was spreading across the earth, was unrepairable. The planet would be uninhabitable in less than five years. The governments knew it was coming for decades, yet they did nothing until it was too late. Now, instead of doing whatever they could to save lives, they were on the verge of nuclear war.

A group of scientists came together and formed the concept of the ship Discovery. It would serve as a record of human life, and a way to preserve a small group of humans. The ship would feature the latest in space pod living, and feature holographic technology, that would create a world that looked just as the earth did, for the regions the groups of people would be taken from. In a sense, they would never know they had been relocated to the ship. There could be no mass hysteria, if the people were unaware they even left their homes.

The real challenge was, to get Patrick trained and the ship completed, before the first nuke was launched. The estimated departure was to come in two weeks. There was no time for error, or unsureness of the new ship's captain. Patrick knew this, as he began to pull on his space suit. Breathing deeply, he was no amateur and he knew it. Lives depended on him.

As the door opened into deep space, Patrick stared out in awe. It was everything he had hoped it to be. His fears were behind him, as a smile crossed his face. He checked his readings one last time, as he floated in the doorway.

"Well, are you going to float there all day, or are you going out?" Pavel teased him.

"I am going out. Oh, and Pavel, don't let anything happen while I am out there." Patrick joked.

"What could happen? There is nothing going on here except space. Maybe the settlement on the moon's surface might drift past as you are finally going out the door."

"I cannot believe we finally settled the moon." Patrick said looking towards the lights on the surface. "Man, that is beautiful."

As Patrick finished his last words, he floated outwards away from the station's doorway. He breathed deeply, as he moved around and saw the earth below him. He didn't know what to think, being so far away looking in. He finally found his strength and courage.

Patrick turned around, and looked back to the moon. The structures were very clear to him from his distance. They looked like a small city, like you would find in some quiet corners of the earth. Except, there were no quiet corners anymore. The days of quiet were gone years ago. They went with the plague that came after Covid. Too many lives were lost, too many mistakes were made. No one knew of the side effects the cure would have.

As Patrick floated deep in his thoughts, a bright light shot in his direction. He struggled to see what was going on. "Pavel, what was that?" He waited, but there was nothing except silence. Then a second blast, and he knew what was happening.

As the moon rattled, and then debris shot into space, a huge chunk of rock flew at Patrick. He pulled at his harness feverishly, quickly moving out of the way. Then as his body drifted in space, he turned and saw the destruction. The moon was blasted in two, separated almost down the center. The lights on the surface, came from nuclear explosions. He was sure of that. "Pavel, do you hear me?"

"Yes, Comrade, it was nuclear in nature. Word is spreading across all channels. There have been explosions back home as well. You are ordered to come back to the station. We are at war. It has begun…the end of life as we know it, is upon us."

Before ☢

"Jon, you have to wake up. Something's wrong" Ellie screamed as she shook her husband.

Jon was a heavy sleeper at the best of times. Ellie wondered what could wake him, when he was like that. She grabbed ahold of his shoulders and shook him back and forth, as the warning alarm sounded from both their cell phones. As a final attempt, she ran into the bathroom, grabbed a cup of water, and threw it at his face.

Jon sat up in the bed, and looked towards her. "What's wrong sweetheart?" He groggily spoke.

"What's wrong?" She screamed. "All hell is breaking loose all around us, and you lay there like a zombie."

Jon jumped to his feet and ran to the window, just as another explosion shook the floor under his feet. He looked out the glass, now covered with ash and debris. Raising the lower half of the window upwards, he leaned out trying to conceal his naked body, just inside the ledge.

Sirens rang out just beyond the road where they lived. Jon shook his head in disbelief. When they had gone to bed, everything was normal. As if normal was something that could be explained, since the virus passed through the United States.

He looked out, as the gas mains in the street lit up the sky with a bluish burst of explosion. As Jon pulled his head inside, he heard the screams, as neighbors ran to their cars, trying to escape the explosions. He wondered, where they thought was safe to run.

Once, he thought they were safe, to move to an out of the way section of New York. He now saw the error of his ways. Jon grabbed his head, and sat on the edge of the bed, as he turned to look at his wife. She sat rocking back and forth beside him, filled with terror, not knowing what was happening.

"Jon, what is all this? What has happened?" She spoke, as tears began to run down her cheeks.

"I don't know. We still have power, maybe we can get some information off the TV or our phones."

"The phones have been blasting an alert for the last hour." She said handing him his phone.

"Why didn't you tell me?" He asked.

"Oh, I don't know. Maybe, I couldn't get your ass to even respond, to me jerking you all over the bed." She screamed, as she gasped for air.

"OK, point taken." Jon lowered his eyes as he took his phone from her.

He looked at the screen, as he clicked the warning alert. As he read the lengthy description, he swallowed hard. In his mind, he didn't see how this was possible. He raised a hand to his mouth, staring in disbelief.

"Well, what is it." Ellie demanded.

"It's two things at once. We are having an environmental collapse, just as war broke out. There have been multiple strike points in the United States. One of those is less than a mile away." Jon said taking her hand in his.

"Wait, this is nuclear? Does that mean we are in danger?" She asked.

"Maybe, but I think it is wise for us to get out of here, as fast as possible, and head away from the blast area."

Ellie stood up and grabbed at her clothes. She looked at her husband standing there completely naked. Shaking her head, she motioned with her hand at his exposed mid-section. He looked down and then raised his eyes to her. Words weren't necessary, he understood.

Racing around the house, Ellie grabbed emergency supplies, and packed whatever food she thought would survive the escape. They had always planned for emergencies, and many of the supplies were kept ready, such as water, a flashlight and batteries. Grabbing a large duffle bag, she piled everything inside.

Jon ran down the stairs, dragging a bag full of clothing and personal items, they could not leave behind. He darted back and forth, grabbing anything he thought was necessary, including the charger cords for their phones.

"Ellie, if there is anything you really want to take with us, grab it now. I have no idea what will happen, but if it is important, bring it."

"I'll look around, but there is only so much we can pile into the SUV. Besides, as long as we are together, I will be alright." She smiled, as she kissed his cheek.

As they moved into the garage, and filled the rear of the vehicle, Ellie looked back into the house. "Be safe, until we come home again. I have spent too many years here, to lose you now."

Turning to get into the passenger seat, she flashed on the 12 years, they had put into rebuilding the house they had called home. It wasn't much when they came there, but together, they made it something to be proud of. She wasn't ready, to have their life in the place ripped away.

Jon made a final sweep, and being sure all the doors were locked, before he came running full steam at the driver's side door. He clicked the garage opener, before stomping the gas pedal and flying out the driveway. He only stopped long enough, to see the door close again, and then he began to fly backwards.

As the vehicle came onto the street, another car came flying towards them. Jon barely got them out of the way, as the vehicle nearly crashed trying to get around. Jon and Ellie looked at each other, as he hit the gas and flew forward. It was time to leave.

The road, was covered with all sorts of destroyed pieces, that were placed there by the explosions in the area. Jon swerved back and forth, as they made their way to a major road. They had both agreed on a direction to go, the only thing they did not imagine was it was where everyone else was headed too.

As Jon slowed the car, in behind the gridlocked road, he looked to Ellie. "What do we do now?"

"I think we are stuck, there is no way of turning around." She shook her head. "Damn, I wish I had a Geiger counter right about now." And then, she laughed.

Jon turned to her in disbelief. She had always found a way to find humor in everything. Then he remembered, that even when she contracted the virus, he thought he had lost her. They separated them from each other, but she hid her cell phone, and called just to calm him, by telling dirty jokes. They survived that experience, but he wasn't so sure now. Maybe, he thought, their good luck had turned on them.

As Jon smiled at her, he felt a rumble from underneath the car. He tried to not act as if he was concerned, then Ellie noticed to. Their eyes met, as they saw each other's fear. Jon turned away and scanned the area, looking off the side of the road, which was empty of traffic.

"It's your call. Do you want to see if this vehicle is worth the money we paid for it?" He asked her.

"I don't think the insurance is worth a hill of beans now, so do it. I want out of here." Ellie's voice was shaky, but her message was clear.

Jon backed up a few inches, and then pulled forward, over and over again, until he was able to leave the road. Changing the vehicle into four-wheel drive, he pulled over the cement edge, and carefully worked his way to the open field just to the side. He was free, and looked for any open area, to head them in another direction.

As they found their way to an old unused dirt road, they had found their freedom. Jon pushed the accelerator, as he glanced back at the cars, who tried to do the same as he did. Ellie looked back through the side mirror, watching intently, as the others tried to come into the field. Just then, the rumbling started again, followed by a blast of light. Ellie stared at the road, as the explosion came, launching several vehicles into the air. As they crashed back to the ground, the explosions came one after another.

Ellie, could not take it anymore, she turned away. The area they had just been in, was leveled in flames, and the people there, were gone in a flash of fire and light. Jon reached over the seat, to where her hand laid, and placed his hand on top of hers. They had escaped, if only for the moment.

Mullins

Chapter One ❂ Six Months Later

Six months on the road, had taken its toll on Ellie. Her nerves were worn from the constant destruction she saw with every stop. She longed for home and friends. Then she wondered if anything she knew still existed. The explosions that blasted around them as they left, surely destroyed everything in their path. Life as she knew it, could not have survived.

"Hey Ellie, you still alive over there?" Jon asked jokingly.

"That was not funny. With all the dead we have seen in the past six months." She was serious in her objection. "God will get you for that."

"Alright, poor choice of words. I get your point. You just seemed somewhere else."

"With all that has happened, I wish, I WAS somewhere else." She said sighing.

"That somewhere else. Am I there with You?" He asked timidly.

"Always. The world might have gone to hell, but we are still married. I guess, we will survive living the apocalypse." She laughed.

Jon looked out of the window of the SUV at the destruction. The road around them was scattered with vehicles, in all states of decay. Some were destroyed months ago, while others still smoked from burning or explosions.

Amongst it all, were the dead, scattered throughout the vehicles, inside and out. Many of their bodies, decomposing in the hot sun. He tried not to look, but Jon could not help himself. The corpses, were once every day people, he thought. The bodies could have been someone they knew once. It did not matter now, they were gone. In this existence, there was no time to mourn the past…or the dead.

Armageddon

As the vehicle swerved back and forth, to avoid the many things thrown about the road, Jon saw a crow, sitting on top of a truck. It studied him, as he came closer. It was as if, the bird was stalking prey. Jon rolled up his window and drove through, trying not to look.

As the bird took to the air, it landed just in front of the SUV, and swooped down onto a dead body. This one, was more intact, than others they had seen. The man must have just died in the last couple of days. His skin was still clean, and did not show signs of blistering from the fallout.

As the bird looked up at Jon again, it immediately threw its head down towards the man's face, and with its beak, ripped out one of his eyes. Ellie turned to see the event, and threw her hand over her mouth. She wanted to vomit, but that would involve opening a window, and she was too scared to do that.

Just as they came close to the bird, it stretched out its wide spanning wings and climbed upwards.

Ellie closed her eyes, and tried to wipe the image of the dead man out of her mind. Jon looked over to her, and then returned his sight back to road, to avoid running over the multiple bodies in front of them.

"Just when I think I get to a place where I can handle all this, I see something like that." Ellie said under her breath, still covering her mouth with her hand.

"Get used to it. I don't think it will get any better in the near future." Jon sounded sad as he spoke. "I guess in time, as the bodies deteriorate, it will get better. Who knows how long that will take."

"I know. Jon, where are we going?" She asked. "I mean, this just seems to be as bad, as the last place we went. It seems like so many dead, and very few living."

"Yeah, the dead do seem to be outnumbering the rest of us. Everything I hoped to see, is gone. And what is left, is changing. It's like nature is taking over from the humans."

"There has to be some kind of safe zones, where people have survived." Ellie sounded desperate as she spoke.

"I just don't know anymore. Try scanning the radio again. Maybe some survivors somewhere are broadcasting."

Ellie turned on the radio, and slowly scanned through the lower bandwidths, and heard nothing. Then she went further, and in her frustration, flew past a sound that blasted for a second. She stopped, and looked at Jon, then smiled. It was like a glimmer of hope.

She moved backwards towards the signal, and there it was again. A woman's voice came through the speakers. She was alive, and broadcasting from a station in northern Pennsylvania. Ellie felt a weight lifting off her shoulders, as she listened. She had not heard another person's voice, except Jon's in months.

"Can you get directions from your phone?" Jon said excitedly.

"If there is still a cell tower, that has power around here. I haven't been able to get a signal in weeks now." She clicked her phone, and let out a yell. "Yes! I have a partial signal. I am getting directions before it goes out."

Jon followed her instructions, as Ellie guided him to the right direction. Through a road covered n death and destruction, they plotted a path towards humanity, or at least they hoped. Ellie smiled for the first time in months. She had hope.

Chapter Two ☢ The Convergence Begins

"Hello my friends, this is Kate Malloy. Still on the air, and still broadcasting for as long as I can. I am, for the most part, still alive after the bombs that went off near here. Radiation is a bitch though. I have to tell you; the world has gone to hell. If you think I am joking, just look out your windows or doors…if you still have 'em. I just got word, a little while ago, that the government is trying to shut down all the radio and TV stations that can still broadcast." She paused to take a drag off her cigarette before coughing and resuming. "I tell you what I say…screw the government. This was all their freaking fault in the first place. I will continue to get the word out to you guys, until they put a bullet in my head."

As they drove the two-hour drive to the radio station. They listened to the woman Broadcaster. She gave information on the conditions around her, as well as, for the listeners who sent her messages about their location. None of it was good news.

Since the nuclear war had broken out, there was death and destruction, in every major city in the United States, and other countries worldwide. The dead were beginning to outnumber the living. Conditions were as bad, as when the virus came, and killed off millions. Ellie remembered the mass graves in New York. She lost too many friends and family, as a president sat idly by.

Jon studied the landmarks, as they made their way eastward. Parts of the road had been cleared. It seemed the more rural the area the less destruction, which suited him just fine. He was tired of dodging bodies and wrecked vehicles. Fortunately, Jon was good at syphoning gas, so the now abandoned vehicles, supplied him better than a gas station.

Up ahead, Ellie saw the sign for Ridgeway PA. They were close, and she was excited. The radio broadcaster had become a beacon of hope. The first hope, they had found since they left home. For once, they found life, instead of a dead body. For that, they were both grateful.

As they drove on, the radio station continued to transmit, and Kate was still on the air. "You know my children; I have been in this game, a long damn time. I have been on the air for nearly 25 years. I have broadcast through everything, including good times and bad. I covered wars, and even Christmases. I must admit, I liked the Christmases more. Five days a week, I have been here." She paused for a moment. "I never thought in all that time, I'd end up covering the end of days. Huh, that is kinda biblical isn't it, but I will not go there. If there is a god, he has forsaken us." She laughed out loud.

As they drove, Kate's voice struck a chord with them. They didn't even know the woman, but still they drove as fast as they could, to be with the stranger who had found a way into their life. Ellie looked down at her phone and saw that she had a full signal. The towers were still active in that area. Her hands shook, as she tried to hit the numbers of the radio station.

"Hello, you are on the air with Kate. Where are you calling from."

"Hello, I am Ellie, we are from upstate New York, heading your way."

"Well Ellie, it is good to hear from you, and I hope you are safe out there."

"We are as safe as we can be. It's just me and my husband Jon. We have been traveling since the bombing started, six months ago."

"Well, bless you sweetheart, and your husband, for surviving so long. I know that was not easy."

"No, it hasn't been, but we are near the radio station now. We are hoping to come and see you."

Kate paused a second, as she looked out the window, at the military vehicles pulling up to the curb, and the soldiers filing out. They had detected her radio station. They were there to stop her broadcast, in any way necessary.

"Listen Sweetie, I don't know how to tell you this, and my other listeners as well." Her voice trailed off for a second. "There are a bunch of soldiers headed into the radio station. I can hear them on the stairs. I think old Kate's days are numbered. To all of my listeners, stay safe and take care of yourselves."

Jon and Ellie turned the corner of the road, leading to the radio station. Kate's broadcast had gone silent, except for the pounding noise on the outer door of her studio. Ellie stared at the radio, as they rolled to a stop on the next street.

There was silence, until Kate called out, and told them to stop. Then a shot rang out, and cut through the quiet of the radio. The only other sound, was Kate's head, as it fell to the desk.

Ellie turned to Jon, with an expression of true fear. She had no words for what was going through her brain. Just then, a military truck rounded the corner. They ducked down, to not be seen as the vehicle plowed through the street, pushing away anyone or anything in its path.

And then it was gone, and they worked up the nerve to go into the radio station. There was nothing left there to help them. Kate lay there dead, slumped over in her chair. She died sending a last message to inform the survivors. 'Trust no one.'

Chapter Three ☢ Survival Of The Fittest

"What the hell do we do now?" Ellie asked, as she looked out over the small town, which was all but abandoned by the living.

"I don't know yet. I just thought, coming here would be the answer. Now, it is like we are back where we started." He said, sounding defeated.

"No, we are not back where we started. We are better than that. We now know, there are others out there who are surviving. And a few, who are being killed off by the government." Her voice trailed off, as she thought of Kate.

Ellie was more than disturbed. She did not even know Kate, but the way she was killed off by their own government, was not right. This did not feel like the country she was raised in.

Assassinations were not done by her own government.

"Are you OK?" Jon said, worried for his wife's mental state.

"Yes. It's just, this does not feel right. Why would they kill her, and not just shut down the radio station and arrest her. I feel like there is something else going on here. Something, they are trying to keep a handle on."

"Then maybe, we need to find out. If for nothing else, to save our lives." Jon's words drifted by Ellie as she was only half listening.

He started their vehicle, and drove down the road, looking at each of the buildings as they moved. There didn't seem to be any signs of life anywhere. Ellie looked into every store front and alleyway. She couldn't understand why Kate would be there, and no one else.

As they drove, Jon saw the dead bodies, that had just dropped in their steps. It reminded him of New York during the virus. People were dropping so fast; they could not bury them properly. Instead, they created mass graves for the bodies, to get them out of the streets and hospitals. In the beginning, the government tried to cover that up too.

"You know, somewhere in these buildings are supplies we might need. Since there is no one here to use them, we might as well stock up." Jon said trying to get Ellie's attention. "Earth to Ellie."

"I'm sorry, there is just a sick feeling in my stomach. You know when I get them, there is usually something wrong. Like, bad wrong." She said looking down.

Jon pulled in front of the grocery store, near the end of the road. The parking lot was still littered with bodies, and the cars of those who died before they could get back to them. Ellie looked, as they passed one by one. Most of the cars were empty. She wondered if the fallout from a bomb had gotten them, or had it been whatever was being covered up.

Jon stopped the SUV, just outside the doors of the store. He thought it better to have a quick getaway spot. He wasn't sure what might be lurking inside. In some way, he didn't want to know what may be inside.

As Ellie opened her door, she stepped out and moved quickly, to avoid the dead body just to the right of her foot. She looked down, at what was once a woman. Now, she was a decomposing corpse, with skin rotting off her bones. 'This one, must have been here a while,' she thought.

Ellie tried to keep down the bile that worked its way up her stomach, and into her throat. The smell was bad, but the disgust was worse. Still, she made her way to the outer door. She just repeated to herself. "This too will pass."

As they moved inside the store, Jon fought himself, from seeing the checkout line as comical. The checkers were still at their stations, some died slumped over their registers. There were customers in line, several still holding to their carts. The grim scenery, was frozen in time, as decay was wearing away at their dead bodies.

"I guess the express lane, is a bad choice today." Jon said jokingly.

"Are you kidding me? That was disgusting. Seriously, you need help. Joking in a situation like this." She grumbled.

"What else do we have. We just can't go on without something, anything to laugh at. We have been too sad and depressed for too long." Jon said, trying to convince her to let go of some of the pain.

Ellie turned and looked at him. Her face changed, and for a moment he thought, from the sounds she was making, that she was crying. She choked and shrugged a couple of times, then covered her face with her hand. The sounds of sobbing grew louder, as she shook back and forth.

"Ellie, please calm down. I didn't mean to upset you. Don't cry." He begged her.

"I'm not crying." She said, as she moved her hand away. "I'm laughing. I get it, I finally get it. I see what you mean, it is funny. They look like mannequins."

"What?" Jon said, as he began to laugh.

They stood their laughing out loud together. For months they had held it all in, now for a moment, they could just be human again. No running to find humanity. No more fear of what was ahead of them. Now, for a moment, a chance to release.

"I am glad you are taking pleasure in other people's deaths." A voice came from out of one of the aisles of the store. "Stay where you are, and you might live."

Jon and Ellie turned around, to see a rifle pointed at them. They looked to each other in fear, not knowing wat was about to happen. The man came forward slowly, as he cocked the rifle in his hand.

Chapter Four ☢ The New Breed

Jon stared hard at the man who came forward towards them. He looked like a mad man, wearing a gas mask, and a deer skull and antlers on his head. He was clad in leather and straps and some sort of old military looking gear. The man looked and sounded crazy. Jon wondered what institution he had escaped from.

"What are you doing here?" The man asked.

"We're not here to hurt anyone. We just needed some food, to help us on our way." Jon said, with a shaky voice.

"This is my store. No one else living, comes here." The man's voice was raspy sounding, as if he did not speak much. The gas mask made him sound even worse.

Ellie spoke under her breath. "He probably killed all the living around here. The man's a lunatic."

"I'm not crazy lady. I am a survivor. And after all that has happened, you have to be a little crazy to exist in a life like this."

"Point taken." Ellie responded to him. "Look, we are not here to take anything from you. We are happy just to leave, and let you get back to whatever you are doing."

The man lowered his gun. He looked them over and then looked back to the store. His mind raced, as he tried to make a decision. Killing them would be pointless, being so many were dead around him already. He could see no positive outcome in more death.

"Take what you need and leave. Just be quick about it."

Jon reached for an empty cart, and grabbed ahold of Ellie's hand. As he pulled her through the store, they looked for food that was not perishable and water. Elie studied the shelves of the store as they walked, and then she saw it. She smiled, as she read the words, 'Blood Orange Tea.' She had become addicted to it before the fall. She couldn't resist grabbing several, and throwing them into the cart before Jon could say no.

As they walked past the magazine rack, Ellie stopped and looked at a newspaper headline. It was from more than six months ago. She smiled, as she looked at the story of the moon colonization, and the ship that left earth just as the bombing started.

"They got away; you know." She said smiling.

"Who got away?" Jon asked, not knowing what she was talking about.

"The ones on the moon colony, and the ship that launched, before all hell broke loose." She said pointing at the image on the paper.

"I wonder if they are still alive? All that new technology, and a first attempt at space travel. Not to mention, when the moon exploded, the colony and half the moon, were hurled into deep space. Anything could have happened." He turned away, not wanting to explore the secret, he had hidden for so long.

"Yes, but I hope for the best for them. They might be the lucky ones, they are probably alive, and look around you. I'd take my chances in space." Ellie said sarcastically.

"Life as we know it may be over, but a new world will arise from it." The man's voice came from down the aisle.

Ellie turned and walked towards him. Jon grabbed at her arm, but she pulled it away from him. She was determined to understand this strange oddity. She walked towards him with no fear. Underneath, she was sure there was some sanity.

"I am sorry for the way we entered your store; it was wrong, and I wish you nothing but peace." She said smiling at him.

"I understand that now." He said, muffled through his gas mask. "You have to be careful with the new world and the undead."

"What do you mean, the undead?" She asked.

"You have not encountered them yet? They are the remains of the mutation. They were human, now the vaccine and the radiation has mutated them. They exist only to feed and kill. You can't reason with them, or negotiate. They have no remorse."

"Have you seen these mutants very often?" Jon asked.

"Yes, and until I got a good look at you, I thought you two were them. I was ready to shoot and not ask questions." The man said, moving his gun over his lap.

"I'm glad you thought about it first." Ellie said sounding relieved.

"It was your laughter that saved you." The man responded.

"Well, I am glad I had a breakdown." She said laughing. "I am Ellie, this is my husband Jon. Are we allowed to know your name?"

"I was once called Isaac, now I just go by I." He said looking agitated.

Ellie watched, as she realized they were overstaying their welcome. She thanked him for the things from the store, and took ahold of Jon's hand. Quickly, she led him back to the front, and to the vehicle.

"It's time to go." Were her only words, as she loaded the food and other items, into the rear of the storage area. She turned, to look one last time to the man, who still watched them from the inside of the store. She waved to him, as she climbed into her seat, and they pulled off headed to the unknown.

Chapter Five ◉ The Undead

Ellie continuously hit the control for the radio. She needed to hear another human voice. Even though their last attempt to find humanity didn't end well, she hoped there were still safe zones somewhere.

As she hit a lower band width, she heard a weird signal come through. She went past it the first time and ignored the sound. Then the second time, she slowed down, and narrowed in on the signal. It came in low at first, then it grew louder. She knew the signal was far off in the distance, if it was so low.

The tone came in more clearly the further they drove. She was sure they were driving towards it. After several minutes of a humming tone, the sound changed, and turned into a chime, before a voice came onto the broadcast.

From the radio, a computerized human sounding voice came through. "Attention all citizens. Philadelphia has been designated a safe zone. It is a safe place, free of fallout radiation, as well as, the undead. These creatures have been eradicated from the safe zone. Be advised, do not approach the undead, they may look human, but they are dangerous and could cause loss of life. The only safe recourse to eliminate them, is to shoot them in the head. This is a public service message from local government services."

Ellie turned to Jon, and thought about what words she could use. "Are those bitches crazy?"

"So that is from a safe zone. Yeah, doesn't sound to SAFE does it?" Jon responded sarcastically.

"Do we really want to go there?" Ellie asked.

"I have no idea. I don't know what is really safe anymore. We could check out the area and decide. Then what do we do, if we go there, and cannot leave if it is not what we think it is?"

"The government has been screwing everyone for years. How do we know, this is not just an internment camp or something?" Ellie asked, trying to hold back her concern.

"Ok, we look and watch, but do not enter. I feel really weird about this. And besides that, why was there a computer on the broadcast, and not a human voice?" Jon could not make sense of it all.

"Maybe, we should have headed north to Canada." Ellie added.

"Wouldn't do any good, things are the same all over. This is a global event, worldwide destruction. Besides, we probably couldn't get across the border. If there are survivors there, then their government is probably trying to control what is going on too."

"Control, that is a good word. More like extermination. They don't want trouble makers, or the undead, as they call them." Ellie paused. "I'm pretty sure they would consider us troublemakers."

"Well, my love, I think we are on our own. At least until we find others who are in the same boat as us.   For now, we drive."

They headed for Philadelphia, for no other reason, than to see what was happening in the safe zone.   Curiosity had the better of them.   Ellie's nerves were on edge, she had no desire to be put into lock down.   The thought terrified her more than anything.   Even with the world going to hell, she had her freedom.

The road through Pennsylvania was much like other places they had been.   It was littered with the dead and crashed vehicles.   There was nothing new, until they reached a larger city.   As they drove by, the road seemed to have been cleared.   Jon slowed a little, and looked around as they passed through.

"This doesn't feel right.   It is all clean.   It's like before the war."   Jon said, staring out onto the road.

"I think we need to get out of here, as quickly as possible."   Ellie said locking her door.

Jon hit the accelerator, as they flew down the road. As they passed a billboard sign, they did not see the police car hidden behind it, or the police officer watching their vehicle. Jon's main goal was to get out of the area, not fall into a speed trap.

As they sped quickly through, the officer turned on his lights and peeled out after them, throwing rocks and dirt into the air, as he launched his vehicle onto the road. He fishtailed the car before straightening up and flying at top speed in behind the SUV.

"Jon, what do we do? Should we stop?" Ellie asked.

"I don't think we have a choice. He is not going to let up." Jon said, as he pulled to the side of the road.

The officer pulled in behind and slowly left his car. Jon tried to get a good look at him through the rear-view mirror, but the man did not stay in a place he could be seen. As the officer came up to the door, he did not lean down or into the window. He just extended a hand, and asked for license and registration. Jon pulled them out, but before reaching them to the officer, he looked at the man's hand which was covered in soars and burn marks. His skin was deteriorating.

Jon leaned over and looked up as the officer lowered his head. Letting out a scream, Jon hit the gas and peeled out from the side of the road. He was terrified at what he saw. The officer's face was ripped clean of flesh, there was nothing but bone, and some shreds of cheek. Jon now knew, what they meant by the words, 'the undead.'

Chapter Six ☢ To Seep, Perchance To Dream

Jon and Ellie flew down the highway, not resting, until they were sure they had lost the undead police officer. Jon could not get the man's face out of his head. For once in his life, he found something to be truly afraid of.

"Are you going to tell me what you saw, or am I going to have to imagine something far worse?" Ellie was desperate to know.

"He was undead…as in, his flesh was coming off his face, he was burned from radiation and who knows what else. I don't even know how he was walking or why. I have never seen anything like this, and I have seen my share of horror films." Jon did his best to explain.

"So, you are saying be afraid?" She asked.

"Yes, be very afraid, and be glad we seem to have lost him. Maybe we can breathe now."

"Not for long. There is the road to the safe zone."

They rolled down the road slowly and cautiously looked ahead to the barbwire enclosed camp. Ellie shook her head and tried to swallow. She knew it was wrong. She could not bring herself to go there.

"Jon, you need to get us out of here. The men inside the gate have assault rifles. If they see us, I have a feeling we will have no choice. Do a U-turn, we have to leave now."

Jon agreed, turned around quickly and headed back as fast as he could. It was no safe zone, they were sure. Jon hit the steering wheel; he was feeling useless in his attempts to save their lives.

"Alright, stop that. We have no time for self-pity or loathing. So, we found about what we were expecting." She found herself venting. "We are alive, which is more than we can say for so many people we have seen on the road. So, what if we couldn't go to a supposed safe zone? We weren't captured by them or zombie cop. We are here and together, that is all that matters. But we need to put some distance between us and here. Then maybe, find a place to sleep."

Jon put his hand over hers. "Yeah, I am tired too. We need to rest and regroup."

After about an hour of driving, they saw the signs for Maryland in the distance. They never intended to go there, but in the haste to get away from the safe zone, they took any direction they could. Just off the road was a motel. It seemed safe and away from everything. It was as good a place as any to stop.

The day had dimmed, and night was approaching. As they parked, Ellie scanned the parking lot and building. There seemed to be no signs of life or activity, except a flickering vacancy sign. Elie smiled as she looked at it, she almost felt welcomed.

As the two got out of the vehicle, they were cautious, after their last experiences. They moved into the lobby, and looked at the keys to the rooms. Oddly, most of the rooms had been vacant to start with. They would have their choice of where to sleep.

Jon stepped behind the counter, where the front desk employee lay dead on the floor. He carefully stepped around, and took the key of a room right beside their vehicle. Elie turned around, and saw the snack machine. She had not seen a candy bar in months, and all she could see was chocolate.

"They should be safe, right?" She asked Jon.

"I don't see why not; they are wrapped and inside an enclosure. Probably as safe as anything."

As she was about to pick up a chair, and bash the machine, Jon came to her side. "Slow down Rambo, here is the key, it was right behind the counter. We need to seriously talk about your need to bash things." He said laughing.

As he opened the machine, Elie grabbed an armful of candy. She smiled at him, because he knew how much she wanted it. She held tight to her armful, as they headed for their room, opened it, surprisingly to find everything clean and untouched.

Ellie could not resist the chance to take a hot bath and remember the feeling of soaking. She found herself trying to drift off, she then realized how tired she was. Emerging from the bathroom, she motioned for Jon to have a turn. She didn't remember how something so simple could help so much.

When Jon came back, they ate and tried to relax inside the safe place they had found for the night. Jon placed a motion activated camera just inside their window, to let them know if anyone approached. Before he could turn and tell Ellie, she was asleep and dreaming.

As Ellie tossed back and forth, she relived the time when they were home. Their old life flooded back, and for a brief moment, her dreams took her to a better place, before the fear and undead reared their ugly head.

Jon watched her in her sleep. He was pleased to see a smile on her face. It was hardly seen anymore. He himself felt calm as well, and it wasn't long, before he drifted off to sleep. The night, for the most part, was peaceful. Until at 7 A.M., the motion sensor went off, and the alarm sounded waking them from their sleep. Someone was there, they were not alone.

Chapter Seven ☢ The Uninvited

"Jon, what do we do. There is no back way out of here." Ellie began to panic.

"Let's just see what is going on first. Maybe the camera went off by mistake."

With Jon's last word, the alert sounded again. There was definitely something moving just outside their door. Jon turned to look at Ellie, and then turned toward the window. He didn't want to give away the fact they were in the room, unless he had to, but he had to know what was outside the door.

Quickly, he moved to the curtain, studying how it could be moved without anyone seeing. Slowly, he placed a hand to the side, and moved it gently, as to not move the whole thing at once. Once he had it open far enough, he looked out and saw nothing.

Jon was puzzled, the camera kept sounding the alarm, but nothing was there. He looked back to Ellie and shrugged his shoulders. He had no idea what was going on. Letting go of the curtain, he looked at the camera in confusion.

"There is no way this thing is wrong. It has never let us down, not in all the time we have had it. There has to be some other reason for the alarms." Jon tried to make sense of it.

"Maybe the battery is low or about to die." Ellie tried to offer ideas, but none seemed right, since the camera had a full charge.

"No, this thing has been plugged in all night to charge. The power grid has not gone out here. There has to be something out…there. Something was moving."

As they looked at the camera, outside the door, they heard a thump. Jon looked up from the camera, and turned his attention to the door. "There's something out there." He spoke. He walked over to the door and looked out the peep hole.

He squinted and looked around, but there was nothing to be seen.

"OK, this is getting stupid. I have to go out there. It is the only way to know what is going on."

"No Jon, it is too dangerous. If there is an undead out there, they will hurt you. Not to mention if the government has come into this area." Ellie pleaded with him.

"Look, just stay here, and get ready to slam the door, if anyone comes after me." Jon insisted.

"And what will you do? I can't do this without you."

"Oh, Ellie, you are so much stronger than you know. I have faith in you no matter what. If anything comes for me, I will run like hell. I promise, I will come back to you. I always come back to you. Now get behind the door."

Jon unlocked the door slowly and quietly. He turned to look at Ellie who was shaking so hard he could see it. He leaned over and kissed her, as he took hold of the handle. "I love you." Was all he said, as he pulled it open and began to run.

Jon flew out of the door, and hit the sidewalk hard. He flew past the SUV and into the open space of the parking lot. As Ellie saw him out the door, she slammed it, and moved to the window to watch.

They both felt their hearts beating hard, but for different reasons. Ellie feared losing the only person who ever made her feel alive. She depended on Jon; he had been there most of her life. He stood by her through loss of family and normal life. He was her rock.

Jon's heart beat so loudly in his chest, he thought it would explode. The running did not make his heart pound as much, as the idea of the unknown did. He was in very good shape. Before the natural disasters started and the war, he was a runner, who did eight miles every day. Then the quakes started with the moon's destruction, that ended the running. He felt he needed to be near Ellie, if the end came.

So far, they had survived, and the quakes had calmed a bit.

Jon stopped running and looked around. He had cleared the area and was safely in the open. Still there was nothing there. He scanned the area all around him, and there was no sign of undead or others.

As he walked back to the door, he looked under the vehicles in the parking lot to see if anyone was hiding, still nothing. His heart slowed its beat, as he realized they were safe. Shaking his head, he began to laugh.

Ellie watched from the window and saw his expression change. She made her way to the door, and opened it, as he came closer. She studied his face, and did not understand why he was laughing.

"Well, what was it?" She asked.

"Nothing…there is nothing here." He said as he tried to stop laughing.

"Well, I am glad you are relieved, but there still has to be a reason the camera went off." She insisted.

Just then, she felt a brush against her leg. Her body went tense, as she tried to tell Jon what was happening. He saw the fear in her eyes as she tried to speak. As he came around the back of the vehicle, he saw it. Down at her shin was a small cat.

Jon began to laugh harder now. Ellie looked at him in anger, being she was too scared to look down at what was below her. She began to fume as he walked up to her.

"Just look down, it's OK." He told her.

As Ellie looked down, she saw the cat. She studied it at first and was hesitant to pick it up. "You don't think it is an undead, do you?" She asked.

"Nope, I think it is just homeless. After all the world has been through, I think it is just as homeless as us."

Ellie bent over and picked up the cat, and took it into her arms. She looked into the cat's green eyes and studied its short grey-haired body. "You are beautiful, aren't you? I guess you are not homeless anymore. You have a home with us."

Chapter Eight ☢ A New Hope

"We need to pack up and get out of here." Jon said, looking at the road just outside the parking lot.

"Yes, but where do we go. We have been traveling so long now, with no direction." Ellie spoke, sounding frustrated.

"I told you before, we keep moving until we find some place safe. I had hoped there would be more than what we have found so far. It just seems there is death and destruction everywhere." As Jon finished his words, he felt the tremor beneath his feet.

"It's another earthquake, isn't it?" Ellie asked, holding tight to the cat who had become frightened of the vibration.

"Yes, it is beginning again. We need to get everything back into the vehicle. Can't afford to be inside, if this gets worse and the roof caves in."

They ran back and forth, moving the few things they took into the room. Elie held tight to the cat, as she collected her things. She wasn't about to let the cat down, in its confused state. She feared losing it. The little bright-eyed creature, was the first new hope, she was able to hold onto in months. She was not about to lose it.

As the last trip was made to take their belongings, Ellie grabbed her stash of candy bars. She looked down at the cat, that seemed to be watching her in amazement. She smiled at it, and said, "It's OK, mama needs these, so I don't kill people." The cat just nuzzled her neck, as if it knew it was safe.

As the vehicle rolled out of the parking lot, Jon looked back. It had been a long time since he had a good night's sleep. The night before was rare and appreciated. He raised his eyes to the road, and he felt the ground beneath them shake harder.

"We can't drive through this. I think we have to let it play out." He said, laying a hand on the cat, and stroking it.

"I don't think we have a choice. We will wait this out, and hope the ground under the SUV does not give way to a sink hole." Ellie said, as her eyes got larger.

"OK, maybe we drive slowly." Jon added, as he put his foot on the accelerator.

"She is calm. Calmer than I would have thought, with all that is going on." Ellie said, holding the cat close to her. "Maybe she came to us, since she saw people for the first time in a while. I bet she is hungry. Next grocery store, we need to get her a supply of food."

As they made their way down the road, Jon watched for signs of life. It had been a while since they saw anything other than the cat. He began to think the road they had taken was a mistake. Along the way, they found a grocery store, and new provisions. The pet food section was stocked, and the cat was set for some time to come.

As they drove, Ellie's mind wondered. "Do you ever think of your family?" She asked.

"Yeah, every now and then. I miss them. I guess they are all dead now, except my sister, Beth. She escaped." He spoke.

"How do you know that?"

"She was on the ship that took off just before the war started. She was a Captain in the air force. Captain Elizabeth Carter…has a nice ring to it, doesn't it. She was recruited for the space program. She wasn't supposed to tell anyone, not even me. I guess she wanted someone to know she was safe." He paused for a moment, and swallowed hard. "Maybe it was my job, to tell the family she made it out alive. I never got that chance. They all died, before I could tell them."

"Why didn't you tell me this?" Ellie said quietly.

"It just hurt too much, I guess. I mean I was proud of her, and all she accomplished. Then there was all the death, and I worried if she would survive in space. When the world went to hell, and the war started, I just shut it out of my head. I am sorry I did not tell you."

"It's OK, I understand why. God knows, we have been through hell. Here's to a little new hope." She said, as she stroked the cat, which had settled down to sleep in her lap.

Mullins

Chapter Nine ☢ Lunch With The Undead

As they drove, Ellie studied a map of the region. She was sure if they headed for a bigger city, there had to be a safe place, that was not overtaken by the government. Pennsylvania seemed to be mostly emptied. She looked downward below Maryland.

"I wonder if the virus, mixing with the fallout, was worse in warmer states?" She said, looking down at the map.

"I have no idea. You would think that a mutated germ, would travel faster in a hot region. And it is the beginning of summer." He stopped for a moment. "I just wish we had more information."

As they continued on, the border of Pennsylvania was coming close. The road they traveled; I-81 went straight into Maryland. Ellie looked at the many farms they were passing. "I could get used to a place like this." She said, pointing to the open farmland. "Doesn't appear to be touched by the bombs or fallout."

"Yeah, it is nice. Problem is, it is open and there is no way to defend, from whatever comes our way." His voice sounded sad, being he too wanted to live in such a place. "I just know, that wherever we settle, this is not over. It will bring what remains, to our door one day."

"I know." She replied. "And when that happens, we will be ready. Then we fight."

The cat sat up in her lap, as if it knew what she was talking about. Turning its head, the cat looked out the window. It was as interested in what was going by, as they were.

"Well, I didn't expect in the middle of the country to see that." Ellie said laughing.

"What?" Jon asked.

"There is an adult book store, just off the road, by that farm. Look at the big trucks parked outside. I guess truckers gotta get off too." She laughed so much; she shook the cat. "Sorry sweetheart, I couldn't help myself."

At the moment they were about to cross the line, Ellie could see in the distance, the line of state police cars blocking the road. She grabbed hard to Jon's arm and pointed. They stared hard, not being able to see, if the men were living or dead.

"Jon, they are arresting people. Look to the side of the road, all the empty cars. They are undead, I swear to it."

"Then we have to get out of here, before they come after us. Hold onto the cat, we are going offroad."

Jon turned the vehicle hard, so hard, that the passenger tires left the road. He had not intended to make so much noise, but the sound carried to the undead blockade. Jon hit the gas, and flew as fast as he could, through a cornfield.

As he drove, the stalks of corn beat at the vehicle, and snapped off in his trail. He didn't know what was in the large field, but he had no choice but to go as fast as he could. Behind, two of the state police vehicles flew after him with sirens blaring. They were dead, but determined to capture their prey.

"Jon, why would the undead need to capture the living?" Ellie asked, not wanting to know the answer.

"Even the undead need a source of food." He said, trying to forget the thought.

"Why didn't you just lie to me?" She asked. "Now, I have that in my head. You have seen too many horror films. It's like those aliens, in the movie mini-series 'V,' from back in the 1980's."

"Now, who is being sick?" He jabbed at her.

"All I know is, I do not want to die like this. I will not be someone's dinner."

"You may not have to. Hold on." Jon said, as he spotted their escape.

Ahead of the SUV was a dug-out section of the property. Jon could see it coming quickly. The property owner was creating a pond on his land, probably for cattle. The land had already been dug deep. Jon looked on, as he was sure it was enough to destroy a vehicle that flew over the edge.

Jon pushed as hard as he could make the vehicle travel. He was lucky to have all wheel drive, a feature, the state police were lacking. They were built for bursts of speed, but offroad was another thing.

Jon was only feet away from the edge, when he veered to the left, leaving the state police cars that tailgated him, to fly over the embankment. One crashed to the bottom, while the other crashed down on top of the first. The impact of the two cars together, caused an explosion from the fuel tanks. As Jon drove, he could see the black cloud of smoke, in his rearview mirror.

"I guess this means Maryland is a mistake." Ellie spoke with a sound a relief in her voice. "I just want to know why everyone we meet wants to kill us."

Jon drove away as quickly as he could, constantly watching for other vehicles. He was hopeful that no one else was following. As they returned to normal road, a blaring siren filled the vehicle. Ellie looked at Jon, she could not believe her phone was back online, and an emergency signal was being received.

Chapter Ten ☢ Toxic Warriors

"What does it say?!" Jon asked impatiently.

"When I know…you will know." Ellie snapped at him.

Ellie looked down at the screen, she had not received a message in so long, it was like learning all over again. She squinted her eyes, and clicked the image on her cell phone. Up popped the message, a warning of impending environmental disasters by region.

"I am glad we did not travel south. This warning says the lower United States is having hurricanes, tornadoes and earthquakes. If anyone is alive there, they won't be for long." She stopped for a moment, feeling sad for any survivors. "We have to stay North."

"I agree, but I wonder how long before these storms rip the planet apart. They just seem to be coming in waves, ever since the moon was split. How long can this go on, before there is a global event?"

"I have no idea. It seems if the government knows, they either aren't talking, or the ones who could tell us, are dead already. It feels like we are living on borrowed time." Ellie looked down, and stared at her newest family member. "It is funny I named you hope. Just right now, I need some real hope.

The road seemed endless, as they traveled back the way they came, trying to find a new path out of the state. As they passed the many farmlands, Ellie looked hard at them. The one thing she noticed was there was something missing…life. There were no people, or farm animals. Not even wild animals were there.

"Jon, even with fallout, why are there no animals? I know we are months out of the danger, we stayed safe and avoided the bombed areas, but where are the birds and whatever? I haven't even seen a squirrel for months."

"The virus did not pass outside humans. So, if anything, it was contamination that would kill anything else. You now, I don't even remember seeing cows anywhere. Could the government be eliminating anything with contamination?" He asked.

"They couldn't do that; it is such a large-scale thing. Come to think of it, how long ago did you see any dead, this far South?" Ellie felt a sinking feeling in her stomach. "They are cleaning this area for some reason. Jon, get us out of here as fast as you can. If you have to take a side road, do it to get us out of sight."

As Jon veered off the main road and took to a country route, he heard the sound of a large vehicle coming down the main road. He slowed for a second to look back. There, crossing the end of the road they had just taken, was an army tank.

"Oh god, that is what is happening, they brought in the army to clear this area. The army has taken over. They have sent out toxic warriors, to remove all the dead animals, and cleanse the place." Jon said, as he hit the gas, and flew down the country road.

"What do you mean 'cleanse the place?'" She asked

"Once the dead are gone, and maybe even the living, then you move in your army, and sterilize the land, before turning it into your new clean home." Jon tried to find the words while fleeing the area.

"You mean they will drop some kind of chemical over the whole place. How can they do that?"

"Easy, just shoot a chemical into the air, and seed the clouds. It is quick and easy, and will spread a chemical as far as they want it to go. What is on the ground, when it rains, gets a wash of whatever germ warfare they choose to use." Jon sounded serious in his desire to get out of the area.

"Drive faster." Ellie demanded.

"Look, this is a winding road. I am doing the best I can, with the conditions I have." Jon said, taking his eyes off the road.

Ellie looked forward, trying to get a grip on her fear. As her eyes returned to the road, she screamed out in panic. Jon looked out, to see what she was looking at, as he hit the brakes hard. The cat jumped, and ran to the back of the SUV as they skidded to the side of the road.

There, in the middle of nowhere, two children sat holding tight to each other. They were scared, and the vehicle flying at them, did not help their situation. Ellie looked at Jon, questioning what to do. They looked around, and there was no one, and no place for someone to hide.

"We have to see if they are alright. They are small kids. Maybe their parents are dead." Ellie pleaded with Jon.

"Ok, but cautiously, and I am taking the gun just in case this is a trap." He said pulling the gun from the glove compartment.

Ellie walked forward and asked the kids if they were alright, but they did not respond. She looked down at them and they seemed healthy. She kneeled down and smiled at the little girl. The child sat there, with her arms wrapped around the young boy, she was protecting with her body.

"Look, we don't want to hurt you. We just want to make sure you are safe." Ellie tried to reason with the girl.

"I've heard that before. That was said, when they took our parents. They never came back." The girl said, with a soft shaky voice.

"Who were they?" Ellie asked. "What did they look like?"

"They were men in uniforms, except they did not look right. They wore masks and safety stuff, but underneath, when they took off the masks their faces were messed up."

Ellie looked up to Jon. Then turned back to the children. "When you say messed up, do you mean like they were burned?"

"Yes, they looked like their skin was missing." The girl spoke, still hanging tight to her brother.

Ellie swallowed hard, and looked back to Jon. "The tank we passed, and your toxic warriors, may just be what is left after the cleanup. We have to get these kids out of here."

"I agree. It's not safe for them." Jon moved back to the vehicle and opened the side door.

"Would you please come with us. I don't think your parents will be coming back. We can keep you safe, but we have to leave now." Ellie tried to calmly convince the children.

As the girl looked around, she thought about what was happening. She also realized Jon and Ellie were healthy and no threat. Just then, Hope popped her head up in the rear window. She was all the convincing the girl needed.

Chapter Eleven ☢ Caravan To Safety

Ellie looked back at the children, as the SUV flew down the country road. She never thought much about children anymore. They had wanted them, when she and Jon had married. As time went on, she wondered why she had never gotten pregnant. Then she got brave enough to visit a doctor, and found out why.

She smiled at them, as she watched their confused faces, look out the windows. The girl Erica, was nine years old and the boy David, was only five. Ellie finally wrangled some information from them, as they drove. Ellie wished she could do something, anything to ease their pain. She just didn't know how. Their parents were dead, and there was no bringing them back.

"They are so quiet." Emily whispered.

"You would be too, if you were in shock from everything they saw. I can't even imagine what they have been through." Jon said, shaking his head.

"So, what do we do now?" Ellie asked.

"What can we do? I think we just got a family, whether we are ready or not." Jon said laughing.

As Jon looked back through the rear-view mirror, he smiled. He had always wanted a family. He had grown up with a sister and brothers. They had been very close at one point, but in time they drifted apart. Jon had hoped for a big family of his own, but when Ellie got the news, he knew it was not meant to be.

As he watched the children, he thought this was their chance, to have what they had been robbed of. He just hoped whatever damage life had inflicted in these children, he and Ellie could erase. One thing he was sure of, in the new world around them, nothing would be easy.

"It's been over an hour. I think we have escaped the toxic warriors." Ellie tried to sound hopeful.

"I'd say so. Look ahead, dead bodies and cars on the sides of the road. We have returned to normal." Jon began to laugh, as he realized this was the new way of life.

As they drove, the cars became more frequent and the dead were everywhere. They knew the area had been bombed. The idea did not sit well with them, fear of radiation still existed. Jon just drove faster, to clear the area. He had a family to protect now.

The radio was on as always, and from time to time, Ellie would scan for any signal. She wondered sometimes why she bothered. It seemed the chance of finding life anywhere was impossible. Still, she told herself, if she didn't look, she would not have found the kids and Hope.

As the radio traveled from empty channel to empty channel, it finally settled on a signal. There was a low hum, that continued to grow. Jon looked down, as he heard some inaudible words, trying to break through the static.

"Jon, there is something there." Ellie said excitedly.

"Yes, but from where?"

The signal came and went, as they flew through the mountainous area. Then a brief line or two came through. The voice over the air said Youngstown, Ohio.

"That is less than an hour from here. I am pretty sure I have seen a sign for it." Jon grew excited.

"Yeah, but do I have to remind you, what happened last time we ran for a radio station, and got our hopes up?" Ellie tried to remain optimistic.

"We have to try. These kids need some kind of safe environment." Jon's face went serious, as fatherhood took over.

"Ok, I agree, let's go to Youngstown."

Ellie looked down to her phone, which had a minimal signal. She pulled up the driving directions and aimed Jon in the right direction. She still had her reservations about running after safety, but what choice did they have.

The radio signal got stronger as they traveled closer. Still, the words that came through, were vague and seemed to repeat themselves. Mostly all they could hear was the location in Ohio. And then, the signal cleared, as they approached the Ohio state line.

"If you can hear this message, please do not crossover the Ohio state line. There has been a massive bomb strike here. It is not safe. Radiation levels are off the charts. If you can hear me, save yourselves. Ohio is not safe. I am recording this message, in hopes that I save anyone, who can hear me. I hope that if anyone is alive out there…." Then the signal began to repeat.

"He must have died while recording. That poor man." Ellie couldn't hide her sadness. "Get us out of here Jon."

Chapter Twelve ☢ A Thief In The Night

"We have to find a place, so we can feed the children and regroup." Ellie was confused, she did not know where to go or what to do, but she had taken on the responsibility of the kids, and she was going to do right by them.

"We need a safe place where there is little chance of anyone being around." Jon replied.

"Head for the lakes, maybe we could find a cabin, or some home that is not used year-round. We might be able to stay there for a day or so, until we sort out what to do. I just need time to wrap my head around what is happening. I mean, we are going in circles and getting nowhere." Ellie tried to get ahold of herself. She was not going to cry, not in front of Jon, she knew he could not handle it.

Jon went silent, he knew not to push the situation. Ellie was at a breaking point, and the kids did not need to see it. He drove through the wooded roads and towards the lakes. If there was a cabin to be found, he was sure it would be in that direction.

About an hour after they left Ohio, John spotted a gas station. He pulled over and scanned the area. The place seemed devoid of life. The only people to be found, were the employee slumped dead over the counter inside, and a woman outside who was getting gas when she died.

The others got out of the car, after Jon gave the Ok. Ellie told the children to wait, until they walked around the building. There was not much to see besides the gas station and a bait shop next door. The place was pretty much abandoned.

Jon went inside and released the gas pump, and prepared to fill up the tank. Inside the store, Ellie looked around for food and provisions. The place was still pretty well stocked. The looters must not have found their way to this area. Then she thought, maybe the looters did not survive in that area.

She found a box in the back of the counter and filled it with whatever nonperishable food she could take. Then, she looked for things they would need for the children. The place actually had some children's toys. Ellie grabbed a few things, being they had nothing but the clothes they were wearing.

Ellie took the box and placed it in the rear of the SUV. Jon was just finishing, as she told him she was heading back inside. He shook his head, as he finished up, and prepared to put the gas cap back on.

Inside, Ellie walked around the counter. Behind, she saw the cash drawer was open. She smiled, as she looked at all the cash inside. She found it funny, that once, that money would have bought so much and given someone pleasure. In the world today, it was useless trash. Nothing could be bought or paid for. Money had no value anymore.

She walked around the inside, scanning every wall and corner, hoping to find anything that would keep them alive or make life easy. Since the destruction, finding the everyday essentials, was nearly impossible.

Walking to the back of the store, she found a door, which she hoped was to a storage area. As she opened it, she saw nothing but darkness. Running her hand over the wall, she searched for a light switch. She was determined to see what was in the room.

Outside, Jon brought the kids into an opening by the lake, and allowed them to move about. They had been stuck inside so long, he wanted them to get some air, even if it was not fresh. As the kids ran and played, Jon joined them, forgetting about the war, and the environmental destruction. Before he knew it, he was having fun. He had forgotten what that felt like.

Jon had not noticed how long they had been running round the side of the lake, and turned back to the building. He did not see Ellie; he had forgotten she was inside. He looked around the front of the building and called out for her, but there was no answer. Ellie was nowhere to be seen.

Jon began to panic; he told the children to stay where they were, and he would be back. Then he headed for the front door of the building. As he rounded the corner, he saw Ellie in the doorway, and as she stepped out, he saw the man behind her.

As they stepped forward, the man raised a gun from behind her. He looked at Jon, and then moved the gun back to Ellie. Jon's heart stopped in that instant, as he heard the shot ring out, echoing through the mountainous area.

Chapter Thirteen ☢ Death

Jon's heart ripped out of his chest, as he heard the gun shot, echo through the quiet mountain air. There was no other sound to block the impact, the winds had died down, and the water didn't even have a ripple. Jon sank to his knees, and threw his hands to his head, as he felt the immense pain run through his body.

He fell back on his heels, as he looked up to where Ellie stood. His life as he knew it, was over. If she was dead, he had no other reason in his mind, to live. Then he thought of the children that had joined them. He was all they had.

Jon looked back to the doorway, as he watched Ellie falling to the ground. He screamed out, as he looked to the man behind her. He shook his head in confusion, as the man also began to fall.

Jon stumbled to his feet, and ran for Ellie. He pulled her up into his arms, and cradled her. She smiled at him for a second, trying to ignore the pain she felt. He struggled to find the words he wanted to say. He never thought this day would come, and now it was at his doorstep.

"I don't understand." He spoke. "He shot you, but why did he fall?"

"He took me by surprise." Ellie whispered. "He was hiding in the back room."

"But, if he shot you, why is he dead?" Jon was filled with emotions, and confusion was one more to add to the list.

Jon looked to the man, and saw his lifeless body. Then as he looked up in the doorway, he saw the answer to his question. Erika walked out into the light, in her hand was a gun. She looked to Jon, and then dropped the gun onto the ground. Her eyes filled with tears, as she moved to Ellie's side.

"You shot him." Ellie said, in a low pained voice.

"I had to. You saved me. You were willing to give me a new life. I lost one mother to a gun. I did not want to lose another." Erika spoke, until her sobbing stopped her from forming words.

"It's Ok sweetheart, you did what you had to do." Jon said, as he pulled her into his arms. "Now, go find your brother, while I take care of things."

Erika ran to find David, as Jon turned back to Ellie. He stroked her hair, and looked at her drawn face. He was no doctor; he didn't even understand how to help her.

"Are you in a lot of pain?" He asked.

"No, just a burning in my side." Ellie answered.

"There isn't much blood. Ellie, how many shots did you hear?" He asked.

"There was only one that I know of."

"I don't think he shot you. I think the bleeding, is from the bullet that passed through him, into you. Maybe that is why you aren't bleeding so much." Jon took hope in the idea, she was not as wounded as they believed.

Jon sat Ellie up, and looked to her, where the blood oozed out through her side. He gently lifted her shirt up, and looked at the tear in her flesh. As he made sure she could sit on her own, he ran into the station. There he grabbed a first aid kit, and paper towels. Quickly cleaning the wound, he saw the bullet had passed through her side, leaving a clean entry and exit.

"I don't know how to tell you this, but I think you are going to be OK." Jon said laughing. The weight of the world had left him.

"What do you mean, I have been shot?" Ellie screamed at him.

"Yes, you were shot, but the bullet Erika used to shoot him, also shot you. He never pulled the trigger. Erika saved your life." Jon tried to breathe, as he explained to her.

"I guess there was some reason to rescue those kids after all. We saved them, and now one of them, save one of us.

Jon explained the extent of the wound to her and cleaned it. He then bandaged her, and stopped the bleeding. Emily turned to him and smiled, as she realized how lucky she was. She was alive, and had finally found the family she had always wanted.

"Send my girl to me. I need to speak with her."

Erika came to her side, and looked down at the ground. "Did I do something wrong?"

"No, my sweet girl, you saved me from a bad man. That is not to say I want you to play with guns, they are dangerous. Just in this case, you did good. Because of you, I might be around a lot longer to raise you." Ellie said, smiling at her.

"Are you going to be my new mom?"

"I'd like to be. Jon and I want to be your parents, and since you have no one else." She barely finished, before Erika put her arms around Ellie's neck.

"Now sweetheart…Where did you find a gun?"

"It was laying behind the counter. I came in the side door to look for you, and saw the man. So, I picked up the gun, when I saw him grab you." Erika explained.

"And who showed you how to shoot a gun?" Ellie asked.

"I saw it on television a long time ago."

Ellie shook her head, at the idea, a child could learn to use a gun so easily. She might have done a good deed, but Ellie still did not feel good about it. In the new world, she thought maybe, guns were necessary to survive.

Chapter Fourteen ☢ Rebirth

Jon looked at the man, in the doorway of the gas station. If not for a child, he would have lost his wife to a stranger's bullet. He shook his head, as he dragged the dead man's body out of the doorway, and into the walkway beside.

David walked up from behind, and stared at Jon. He was too young to understand. Jon did not have the words to explain the situation to such a small child. Instead, he looked David in the face, and spoke. "Everything is going to be alright; I promise."

As Jon lifted the boy into the air, David wrapped his arms around Jon's neck. Without even a thought the boy said. "Thanks, Dad." As David buried his face in Jon's neck, the boy could not see the tear run down his cheek.

Walking back to the vehicle, Jon placed the boy in the back seat, where he curled up with a blanket and went to sleep. Erika was not far behind; it had been a long day for everyone.

"Did you find anything in the back room besides our dead friend?" Jon asked.

"Yes, I did. It is full of horded supplies. We could fill the back of the SUV with all of it. Best of all, there are things we need, from food to water, to pet supplies. There're even some kid's clothes back there that might just fit these two." Ellie's mood had lightened since the threat of her death.

"You feeling alright now?" Jon asked her.

"Yes, I am." She said looking into the back seat of the vehicle. "And that, makes me feel so much better."

"Yeah, I know. The world is going to hell, and we all end up together. There just aren't words." John said, as he headed into the station, to pick up the supplies.

As the kids slept, Jon pulled out onto the highway. The road ahead, seemed a little brighter than before. They drove around the lake, and scouted the many places, that were once luxury vacation homes.

Driving along, they looked for any people who might still be living there, and the undead who might be remnants of the war. The place seemed dead, but in a good way. It was off season, and people had not had a chance to come there yet, for vacation or summer time.

As they came to the end of the road, they saw a chalet style house, and Ellie's eyes lit up. She had always loved them. She never dreamed they could own one. Turning to Jon, she looked at him, in the way she had always, when she wanted something. He did not have to ask, what was on her mind.

They pulled up the drive, being cautious of who or what might be lurking inside. They saw no one, but then again, they saw no one at the gas station. Jon parked the vehicle and walked towards the building. Calmly, he knocked at the door, but there was no answer. Then he looked through the windows, there was no one, not even a dead body. He breathed a sigh of relief. He did not relish the idea of cleaning up the dead.

Jon paced back and forth, wondering how to get inside. Walking up to the porch, he looked down at the welcome matt. He wondered, if anyone still left a key, in such an obvious place. Lifting the front corner, he had his answer.

As he lifted the key to the lock, it turned, and he gained access to the house. Inside, he made his way, room to room, searching for any signs of recent tenants. He found none.

The place had been empty, for some time. Jon wondered if anyone had been there since the war. He smiled as he looked at the furniture. They would not be sleeping on the floor that night. Jon headed out to Ellie, who had started to wake the children.

"Are we safe here?" She asked.

"Yes, we are, and the place is furnished. You have to see this." He said happily, putting an arm around her.

They unloaded the things they needed, and placed them inside, as Jon began to set up a security perimeter around the place. He had been caught by surprise before. He was determined to not let it happen again.

Chapter Fifteen ☢ Army Of The Undead

Jon ushered the children into the cabin, and waited, as Ellie made her way in to look around. She seemed happy, happier than she had been in some time. Jon looked out and studied the tree line. He was cautious, but he had been cautious since the war began.

As he looked back to the house, he smiled, Ellie had gotten her wish for a house with kids. For a moment, this was her dream. Jon worried, because he knew sometimes, dreams turned into nightmares. He put the thought out of his head, as he walked through the door.

The area around the house was all woods. So many trees, and so many hiding places, for the living or the undead. Just as Jon was out of sight, the sound of twigs breaking, echoed through the darkened landscape.

There was no living thing, to hear the cracking, that went down like a set of dominoes. One place after another, the cracking went in sequence. Inside the house, no one heard a sound, and that was by design. The house, blocked quiet sounds, for the luxury of rest and relaxation. Outside, the darkness masked the figures, that moved on all sides of the forest.

As the daylight dimmed, all that could be seen were the red pin points of the mounted lights of rifles. Looking around, the red dots filled the area. They numbered in more than thirty. The undead had gathered an army, to hunt the only living in the area. They waited like wild animals, stalking their prey. As men, they were human, as the creatures they had become, predators.

Inside the house, Jon went about his normal setup. He was proud of his security routine. It had kept himself and Ellie alive for months, when so many they had seen, had already died. Even though he thought there was no one to be seen, Jon still felt the anxiety. The cameras had a purpose.

"Why are you bothering with that?" Ellie said, staring at him as if he was paranoid.

"Look, I know we are out in the middle of nowhere. I should let my guard down, but I can't do this. I cannot forget, a man came from nowhere, and you were shot." Jon said, becoming frustrated.

"Ok, I get it. And yes, I think you are right. I just wish we were in a situation that this was not needed." She sighed, as she looked down at the security devices.

"Ellie, I wish we lived in a world that this was not the norm. In the world that is developing, we have no choice, but to protect ourselves. Not to mention, we have two children now, who need us. If we get killed, then who will look after them. I mean, hell, we found them wandering on the road like discarded puppies."

"That is a hell of a way to look at it. Trouble is, I cannot see another way, to describe it better. I'm sorry Jon, set up your cameras, and any other security you feel necessary. I admit, I am wrong on this one. The world has gone to hell, and we have to survive." Ellie said, turning to go to the children. "I am going to make sure the kids aren't running wild. Maybe I can get them into a bath, and some clean clothes."

Ellie found the children sitting in an upstairs bedroom. She looked through the door, and watched for a second, to see what they were doing. As she looked on, there was nothing. They did not talk or play. There was no jumping on the bed, like a small child, they just looked forward in silence.

The scene scared Ellie for a moment. She wasn't sure what they were doing or why, but she entered the room and sat down beside them. Still, they did not say a word.

"So, what are we looking at?" She asked.

"Nothing." Erika answered.

"Then, why are we sitting here like this?" Ellie asked.

"We don't know what to do." David answered, in a shy quiet voice. "What would you have us do?"

"Nothing, sweetheart. You are free to do as you wish."

"We have never had that kind of freedom before." Erika said to Ellie.

"You can play and be kids. I even brought some toys for you to play with, and clean clothes. I thought maybe after a bath, you could have some play time."

"We never did that before." David said, staring at the floor.

"Well, maybe it is time you learned to have some fun." Ellie said, as she looked into the adjoining room at the bathtub. "If I can get some hot water going in here, we will start with a bath."

Ellie looked around the room for soap and towels. The place was well stocked, and the bathroom was very clean. She pulled everything together on the counter, and brought in the clothes that she had for them in a box. She looked down, for a world falling apart around her, she had done well by them.

"Alright, who is first?" She asked, as the children sat looking through the doorway. "Ok, not both of you at once. Look, this is for both of your benefits. I am sure under all the dust and dirt, are some beautiful children."

Erika stood up, and moved to the door, looking scared. She looked in, as the tub filled with water. They were in luck, not only did the power work, but the hot water as well. Erika came to the side of the tub. She acted as if she had no idea how it worked.

"What's wrong, have you never been in a tub before?" Ellie asked.

"We never had running water in the place where we lived. It wasn't big, or nice like this. It wasn't a house at all, more of a camper." Erika tried to explain.

"You mean, you and your parents, lived in a camper?" She asked.

"Yeah, I think that is what they called it."

"You poor baby. I guess, you would not have running water. Well, you are in for a treat. This is something you will learn to like."

Ellie helped the girl pull off her shirt. As she moved behind Erika, she saw the scars that covered her back. Ellie swallowed hard, as she realized the child had been beaten regularly. These scars were not new, and not from being on the run. It took years to build up the scar tissue that covered her. For the moment, Ellie did not feel so bad for the death of the children's parents.

Mullins

Chapter Sixteen ☢ Pretty Lights On The Wall

The children had their baths, and Ellie gave them new clothes to play in. The children had taken quickly to the idea of the bathing. As soon as they finished, Ellie saw a change in them. The children seemed to relax. They had learned to trust her.

Ellie thought about the scars and bruises, that both children bore. She could not imagine being so young and enduring such pain. They were tougher than she thought. She had known adults who would have died under less punishment. Ellie smiled at the idea, she would give them more love than they had known, no one would hurt them again.

Ellie went about cooking dinner. This was something that had not happened for her or Jon for months. They usually grabbed food and ate on the run from one disaster or another. To sit down to eat a real meal, was a thing of the past.

Ellie called the children to the table and Jon joined them. Sitting there, the children once again sat silent. They had never done this before. Ellie watched, and soon discovered they had so much to learn. She walked them through each step of table etiquette. It was a bit rough going in the beginning, but when they got a taste of real food, they were more cooperative to learn.

Jon watched the children, and figured out for himself there was more going on than he knew. After they had eaten, Ellie explained it all to him. Jon ran his hand to his mouth, as he realized what the children had endured. He could not imagine how a person would hurt a child like that. Then he looked to them. His instinct to protect, kicked in as he quickly adopted the role of father.

The children moved to the couch and sat staring at the television. They had never had one before. As Jon went to their side, he reached up, turned on the set, and looked to the side where DVDs were collected. He smiled, as he found a cartoon about a famous bear. He put it in, and started the movie. The kids sat up, and immediately took to it.

"Good move." Ellie called out from the kitchen, as she washed the dishes.

"Yeah, well, you can't go wrong with a classic. Besides, I thought they needed something to continue the good mood you started upstairs." He said laughing.

"All I did was give them baths, which might I add, they needed badly. That was some dirty water draining from that tub. Speaking of which, if you want to jump in quickly for a shower or bath, I am good here."

"Are you trying to say I stink?" Jon said, smelling his clothes.

"Yeah, a bit, but that is the way it works these days. So, have at it. I am done with running water. I will just join the kids on the couch."

Jon smiled, as he bounced up the stairs, headed for his clothes and the bathroom. The hot water felt like a miracle on his skin, as it dripped down from his head, making its way down his back. He had always tried so hard to watch out for Ellie, that he missed out on the few opportunities for hot water. This moment, was a reward, for his hard work.

As Jon ran the washcloth over his body, he admired the muscle tone he had developed, being on the road. He seldom ate things that were bad for him, and the better eating made his muscles more toned. Before the war, he never had enough time to work out because of all the hours of work. Now, he was impressed.

He looked down at the water, as it splashed around his feet. He wondered what living like this every day would be like. Hot showers and good meals. A warm home, with working appliances. Even the woods around, seemed welcoming at first sight.

As John stepped out of the tub, he pulled the towel around him. It smelled good, like dryer sheets with a scented smell. He enjoyed the feeling of being wrapped in something other than his clothes. He moved around the bathroom naked, feeling the air on his skin.

As he stopped to wipe the steam from the mirror, he looked at his face. He had a beard these days, it was easier than shaving while on the road. He liked the more rugged look he had attained. A positive thing he had gotten from the war, he thought. For a moment, he found a bit of relief from the harsh life that was forced upon him.

After getting dressed, Jon made his way down the stairs. He came up behind the children, who were laughing and sounding normal. He was not prepared to see them like that. They were for lack of better words, normal.

Ellie turned to Jon, and smiled. "My, don't you look good."

"I feel good. I feel clean and relaxed, for the first time in a long time." He said laughing.

"So, kids, I take it you enjoyed the movie." Ellie asked.

They both agreed, starting to play back and forth with each other. The place and the environment had done the trick to loosen everyone up. None was uptight or scared. No one was prepared, when the first camera alarm went off.

Jon turned and looked to the camera, as the kids were distracted, looking out the large glass windows in the rear of the house. They got up, and walked over, staring that the light show that appeared with many small red lights. Erika turned to Jon. "It is like Christmas, with all the lights. It is supposed to happen in winter."

Jon turned to see the lights, as he screamed to the children to get down. The first bullets hit the window above where the children stood. Ellie grabbed at the kids, dragging them towards the lower level, which had no windows. Jon cautiously looked out, as he saw the army of red lights, headed towards the house. They were trapped, there was no way out. The Undead had arrived.

Chapter Seventeen ☢ No Escape

The bullets flew through the air, making screeching noises, as they tore holes in the building. From all sides, the mutated army shot, not showing concern for the lives inside. They had a goal in their assault and it did not require everyone to live.

Jon fell to the floor, crawling his way out of the exposed glass windows, which much of them were now scattered on the floor. He didn't dare raise his head, to see how close the shooters were. He was terrified, his life as he knew it was probably over.

As he crawled past the kitchen, he looked to the hall with its lack of windows. He was close enough to the basement steps, to make a run for it. As he stood up, the shooting increased. For a moment, he thought they could see him. As he reached the top of the stairs, a stray bullet buzzed past his shoulder, scraping across his skin. He stopped long enough to see the blood flying out. He grabbed onto the wound, and applied pressure as he stumbled down the stairs.

"Jon!" Ellie screamed. "Are you alright?"

"Yeah, it grazed me. I just need to cover it and stop the bleeding."

Ellie ran for the lower bathroom and found the first aid kit. She sprayed the skin with medicine and wrapped a gauze bandage around the area, and taped it off. The blood seemed to be contained within, as she looked to see if there was anything else she could do.

"Might not be perfect, but it does seem to be doing the job. Jon, why are they shooting like that. What could we have done, to have made them come for us?" Ellie struggled for her words.

"I don't know what they want. It is almost as if the mutants want something we have."

"Like what?" Ellie spoke slowly as she looked to the children, who sat quietly staring at the wall. "Oh no. It can't be. They don't want us; they want the children. When we found them on the road, maybe it wasn't their parents that had lost them, maybe it was the army."

Jon moved to the children and looked down at them. They did not seem to be all that affected by what was going on. They just sat there in the trance state, Jon and Ellie had witnessed before.

Jon put his hand on Erika's shoulder as he spoke to her. "Have you been taken by these men before? Did you escape from them?"

"You mean the ones with the messed up faces?" She asked.

"Yes, I am pretty sure they are what we are talking about." Jon said, trying not to pressure her.

"Yes, they took us when our parents died." Erika answered.

"Did they kill your parents?"

"Yes, then we went with them to the big building, where they took our blood." Erika said, looking scared.

"What did they do then?" Ellie could not hold back any longer.

"They said we had to have a lot of tests. It hurt when they did things to us, so when the nurse was busy, we ran away."

"The place was near here?" Jon asked.

"It was near where you picked us up." Erika said, as she started to cry. "Don't make us go back there, please."

"Don't worry. If we can get out of here, you don't have to go back. Trouble is, getting out." Jon said, listening to the bullets as they slowed down, and then stopped.

"Why is it all quiet?" Ellie asked. "What are they up to?"

"I am betting, they are coming in. And, I am sad to say, we have no options. There is no way out of here alive." Jon stood up and turned to look up the stairs. He could hear the footsteps outside on the ground, as the mutated creatures ran towards the doors to the house.

Jon reached for the gun; he had carried since the gas station incident. He opened it up, and saw he had four bullets. He lowered his eyes, knowing that would make little difference against an army of the undead. His heart beat faster, as he tried to find any idea, or way they would survive the situation.

As the front door broke free, and the soldiers started to come in. Jon knew, there was no way he could save them. He put himself in front of Ellie and the kids, and waited for the soldiers.

Mullins

Chapter Eighteen ☢ The Chosen Ones

As the soldiers filed in, they headed down the stairs. Their targets were right in front of them. As the soldiers drew in close, Jon stood his ground. He wasn't about to back down, even in death.

"What do you want?" Jon yelled at the lead soldier, who came in close to him.

"I am sure you figured it out by now. You have something we need, the children. They seem to have some kind of immunity to the virus. If we can test them and get a cure, it is one step closer to survival." The soldier said, staring into Jon's face.

"The virus doesn't matter; it is the fallout that is the real killer here. Besides, they are just kids, isn't there any other way to test? Is there no other immune person?" Ellie blurted out.

"Doesn't matter if they are kids or not, we have to survive. Living or dead, they will be tested. And if you get in our way, you might not live either." The soldier took a step closer to Jon and pushed him out of the way.

Ellie stood her ground as the man put his deformed face into hers. His skin was shredded, and pieces had dissolved due to radiation poisoning. Many of the other soldiers had similar markings on their skin. They all looked like their bodies were covered in soars. They were truly the walking dead and did not know it.

Ellie studied the man in front of her, and wondered if he was still human at all. His body had changed so much, it reminded her of someone from an old zombie movie. She wondered if this was how the human race would end, in a mutated state, with no hope, but to die off piece by piece over time.

The man raised his hand and stroked her blond hair. He admired her beauty. He had not seen a real woman for some time. Ellie stood her ground;

she would not let him see her be scared. As the man drew closer, she trembled and held back on the urge to scream.

"You know, you don't have to die. You could come with me. I could be very good to you. You would get used to me in time. Just close your eyes, and don't look too much at my skin." The man taunted her.

"There are a lot of things I want to do with the rest of my life before I die. And being with a mutated freak like you, isn't one of them." Ellie said, as she screamed in his face.

"Fine, have it your way. Kill them." The soldier ordered.

As Ellie moved back to the wall, Jon was thrown in her direction, as well as the kids. Jon stood up and looked at her. He was proud of the way she defended herself, he expected no less. She was, and would always be a fighter.

The soldiers filled into the room and lined up, rifles in hand. Just as the soldier was about to give the order to fire, his radio went off. "Don't kill them, we may be able to run tests on the adults as well." The soldier turned and motioned for the men to lower their rifles.

"I guess you lucked out. Today you live. Not that living will be so good, with all the testing you will go through. Maybe…eventually, you will beg me to kill you. Or maybe, you will change your mind and realize I'm not so bad after all." He said, as he ran a hand down Ellie's neck.

Ellie could not contain it any more. She was enraged that he had touched her. She moved forward, all the time staring him in the face. She put her hands on his shoulders, and he smiled, as he looked her in the face.

"You want my attention, don't you?" She whispered in what was left of his ear. "Then you will get your wish." She laughed, as she rammed her knee into his crotch, and he doubled over in pain, on the floor. "You said you wanted attention, now you got it."

Another soldier came to grabbed Ellie and Jon, and led them out of the house. Outside, a military truck awaited them. As they climbed in, the children were already onboard. They were sitting, like they had so many times before, just staring in front of them. It was as if they were leaving their bodies.

"Children, are you Ok?" Ellie said, as she made her way to them.

"It's all happened before. We are used to it. It is a part of life now." David spoke in an emotionless tone.

Ellie turned to Jon. "This can't be happening. Isn't there anything we can do to stop this?"

"We have been lucky for so long. Maybe our luck has just run out. It had to happen sooner or later." Jon said, as he sat beside the children, looking off into space.

"No…no damn way are we going down like this. We wait until they take us to wherever, and then we fight. I have lived too long, and struggled too much, to die this easily." Ellie was enraged, and if no one else would save them, she was determined to do it.

Chapter Nineteen ☢ Just Like Lab Rats

The truck pulled up to the outer gates of the facility. The outer walls were covered in barbed wire, and looked to have a deadly current running through them. The grounds were well guarded, visitors were definitely not welcome.

As the soldier looked out to the guard shack, the gate began to retract. They were expected. The truck moved inside, and drove up to the large building, that appeared to be under lockdown.

From inside, a group of scientists moved out to the back end of the truck. They did not speak, as the soldiers went about their business of retrieving the test subjects. There was no fight, as the four were lined up to be examined.

As the scientists walked back and forth, they observed each one individually. Ellie watched, trying to get a clue what they were up to. She had trouble reading them, as they all wore sunglasses. She couldn't understand why, being it was getting dark.

They were led inside, where the children were separated from them. Ellie pulled her arm free, from the scientist that was examining her. She did not want to let the children out of her sight.

"No need to fight. They aren't going far away. They are just going to be sterilized for our protection. They might have germs, that would harm us." The female scientist spoke, as she looked over Ellie's body.

"What do you want from us? You can't believe we offer some sort of cure for what has happened to you." Ellie wanted answers.

"We believe there are some who are immune, and perhaps a vaccine, would slow the rate of degeneration in us, or stop the deaths of others in the future."

"I hate to tell you this, but a vaccine is not going to save you." Ellie blurted out.

The scientist moved closer to her and took off her glasses. Her eyes were drawn in, and darkness surrounded what was left of her eyes. She smirked as she looked at Ellie. The scientist was jealous of her features, and the fact she was still beautiful.

"Don't you see, I know there is no saving myself. I was beautiful once, just like you. Then I was exposed to the virus and then radiation. It's a wonder I am still walking around here. I know I am going to die. If my experiment gives me just a few more days, then it is worth it." The scientist spoke, with a sound of disgust in her words.

"Don't you understand, you are harming those children with your tests. They are already scarred physically, and being here is screwing with their heads." Ellie pleaded with her. "If there is any humanity left in you, please let them go. Let them have some resemblance of a normal life."

The scientist looked towards Ellie. Somewhere deep inside, she heard what Ellie was trying to say. She fought herself and her need to do her experiment. She was torn, but she did not know wat to do.

"You know, the children are not the only ones who are immune." She said, as she looked down at her equipment. "I believe you have the same factor in your blood as well. It would explain how you have gone so long without being infected."

"Then keep us, but let the kids go free." Jon pleaded with her.

"Those kids would not survive but a few days on their own. They would be dead from lack of food and protection. Not to mention, what the undead would do to them. They are, what I would call prey, for the vicious animals, we have all become. They will need protectors to lead them into adulthood."

"What are you saying?" Ellie began to see a ray of light in the situation.

"If you help me with the experiment, I will allow you, and the children to escape."

"How can we trust you?" Jon asked.

"You have no reason to. I am just a scientist, who has her own agenda."

"I am Ellie, and this is my husband Jon. What is your name?"

"Before the end of normal civilization, whatever that was, my name was Laura."

"OK, Laura, what do you need from us, to use in your experiment?" Jon asked.

"Simple, I just need two completely separate blood draws. One from each of you, so there is a difference in blood types and properties. If I get it, I do not need the children. Truthfully, I do not think they can help any more, than they already have in the past." Laura said, with a grim look on her face.

"You mean you took their blood, and it didn't help?" Ellie said, trying to understand.

"We used their blood, and tried to formulate a vaccine and administered it to test subjects. Only thing is, it backfired and in a couple of cases, made the degeneration increase. I asked for the army to find the children, in hopes of trying for another cocktail. I had no idea you two even existed. Maybe as adults, you have some other abnormality in your blood, that makes you unique."

"How long after we give blood, could you get us out of here." Jon knew the sooner they were out the better. There was no way, he wanted to give Laura, a chance to change her mind. He looked her straight in the face and awaited her answer.

"If I take two pints of your blood, you may be nauseated, dizzy, or light headed. If I get some sugar into you and some juice, you should be able to run in a few minutes. You just have to be careful and not overtax your bodies, until they compensate for the blood loss. It looks like both of you have been injured, I can put an antiseptic on that as well, to help you heal."

"OK, take our blood. Let's get this over with. We need out of here, before anyone else figures out what you are doing." Jon insisted.

Laura set them both up with blood draws. It took over a half an hour to draw from both Ellie and

Jon. As they sat there, Laura treated their wounds and dressed them, better than they had been before. When they were done, she put a patch over their needle marks, and gave them sugar loaded candy and drinks, to boost them back up.

"I'm going to get the kids. Get as much of that in you as you can. You are going to need it." Laura said, as she left the door.

"You trust her, don't you?" Ellie asked.

"Do we have a choice?" He replied. "We have to get the kids and get the hell out of here."

Laura made her way down the hall and into the lab, where the kids waited after their exams. She walked in calmly and took custody of the kids. Then she slowly led them out the door and down the hall. They did not fight her, they just looked ahead in their comatose way.

Laura grabbed onto both of their hands, and drug them quickly down the passageway, and into the medical lab. Inside, she reunited them with Jon and Ellie, who were prepared to leave. Erika looked up in surprise, as she realized they had been reunited. Their family was back together again.

"There isn't time for a big reunion. We have to get out of here." Laura said, looking nervously out of the door. She led them to the outer exit and to a secret underground tunnel. They ran hard and fast towards the outer opening.

When they arrived, Laura used her card key to release the outer door. She looked down at the children, and then to Jon and Ellie. Her only words were, "Be safe and run."

Laura watched as the four figures faded into the darkness of the woods. And then they were gone. As Laura turned to head back down the tunnel, she heard the footsteps approaching from the rear. She had accomplished her goal, but was caught in the end.

"You let them go, didn't you?" The bearded man fumed.

"Yes, they got away, but in my lab, there are four pints of blood with a possible antidote." Laura tried to excuse her actions.

"It's too bad, you have proven we cannot trust you." The man said, as he turned to the guard at his side. "You know what has to be done."

"No! Wait!" Her words rang out, as the sound of a single bullet tore through the air, discovering its mark.

Mullins

Chapter Twenty ☢ Recovering Hope

The light faded, as they headed deeper into the forest. Ellie held tight to the children, as she dragged them behind her. Jon did his best to keep up, only to fall victim to his head spinning. He had to stop; his body was not cooperating. He called out to Ellie, just before he doubled over.

She spun around to look at him, just as he opened his mouth and spit forth everything in his stomach. They had been warned about the effects of giving the blood. Ellie was fine, it did not seem to affect her, but Jon had not eaten as much and he was thinner than she was.

Ellie walked over and placed a hand on his back. She felt bad for him, but now was not the time to be weak. Weakness would get them captured again. They did not know if soldiers were after them or not, but Ellie was not going to allow a round trip back to the science lab.

"Jon, I love you, and I know this is hell on your body, but we have to go." Ellie spoke, as she tried to lift him to his feet.

"I know, I just had to get it out of my stomach. I was cramping. I am OK now. Do you know which way we are going? We need to get back to the house." Jon said, catching his breath.

"I am sure we are heading parallel; with the road we came in on. Are you sure we should go there? What if they come back looking for us?"

"We need transportation and our things. And, somewhere in that house, Hope is hiding, waiting for us to collect her." Jon finally got his breathing under control.

"With all that was happening, I forgot about her. If they hurt the cat, I am going back to that compound with bombs." Ellie had become angry.

They ventured for an hour before finding their way to the road, that turned off to the house. Jon walked a little faster when he saw the place. His concern grew, for finding anything alive inside, with all the bullet holes. As he walked past the SUV, he looked around for damage, luckily there was none. The soldiers might have been toxic, but their aim was good.

As they approached the front door, Jon stopped Ellie. "You need to stay here until I go inside."

"Why can't we all just go in?" She asked.

"Because inside, there might be something children should not see." Jon's face told of how he was trying to protect them for the possibilities.

"Be careful." Was all Ellie said, as she led the children back and sat them in the vehicle.

Jon walked inside, and saw the holes in the walls, illuminated by the light of the full moon. Even with the surrounding trees, it shone through like a beacon. The house lights that were not shot out, helped with is search. Jon started upstairs and looked under all the beds, and then throughout the bathrooms and kitchen. The cat was nowhere to be found.

Jon was giving up on hope, as he walked downstairs, where they were captured. His mind raced, with the images of the half dead soldier touching Ellie. He felt the anger within him rising. He had to watch helplessly as it all played out. He knew if he interfered, the soldier would have killed her. Still, it did not make him feel any better.

As he sat down on one of the chairs that was still in one piece, he tried to regain his composure. He reached for a bottle of water, he had brought with him, as he began his search. Slowly he sipped it and swallowed hard. His throat was still raw from the acid he threw up.

Then down at his leg, he felt a gentle brushing feeling. At first, he thought he had imagined it, and then the rubbing came repeatedly and more forcefully. Jon looked down, and there was Hope, trying to get his attention. Then Jon remembered, the cat loved water from a bottle.

He picked her up, and cradled the cat in his arm. "I am so glad you are safe little one. I guess you want my water, don't you." Jon took her up to the kitchen, and found a clean bowl, that had not been destroyed, and gave her some of the water.

As the cat drank, he went to the door and let Ellie know everything was OK. She looked relieved as she turned to tell the kids everything was alright. Ellie could breathe again after all that happened, they were all together again.

Jon quickly swept the place and took everything out to the rear of the vehicle and piled it in. Then he and Ellie took turns looking for anything they could salvage from the wreck of a house. As they finished, they stood out front, as Jon pulled the cat in close.

"For a brief moment, this was as close to home as I could have dreamed." Jon whispered, feeling the cat, lean in and begin to purr.

"I know, I felt it too. But you know, it will happen again. I just feel it. One day, we will find a place that is not surrounded by an army of the undead." She barely got the words out, as she broke out laughing. The whole situation was insane to her. She wondered how the world had ever come to the state it was in. She was sure, if the natural disasters did not kill them, then the remains of human life on earth, did not stand a chance either.

Chapter Twenty-One ☢ You Can't Be A Beacon

As the SUV backed out of the driveway, Jon stared at the bullet riddled exterior, of the house. "It could have been so nice here." Ellie just sat in her seat, as a rush of emotions, came over her. She hadn't dared to get too attached to the place. It was all too easy she thought, and in the life they had been forced into, easy was not the way it was.

Ellie looked around into the back seat, where the children were playing with their toys. She had trouble believing these were the same children, who had earlier gone into the zombie staring phase. She wondered if the way they were captured, and their parent's deaths, had conditioned them to lock out the world around them in these situations. Whatever the case, she was happy they seemed to be normal for now.

"Where do we go now?" Ellie asked, as she turned back to look out of the front of the vehicle.

"Somewhere far from this sterilized space. We need distance, so they cannot find us again." Jon answered.

"And where would that be?" She laughed.

"Anywhere but here." Jon tried to be serious.

"I think we need a safe undead free space, where we are not looking out for fear of others. Maybe we can be a beacon and gather the wanderers together." Ellie knew her idea was risky, but it was the best one they had.

Jon sat motionless for a few minutes. He ran it all through his brain. The harder he thought, the more reasonable it sounded. He turned to her and smiled.

"Not bad at all."

"You mean, you agree with me?" She asked.

"Yes, I do. It beats running all over the remains of the United States, looking for some kind of safety. I say we create our own, and find those who are looking, just like us. We could broadcast a message to them, and not let the government zoom in, like they did before. There has to be a way to let people know there are still fallout virus free zones."

Ellie got excited at the idea. "We need real doctors, to test those coming in. We want to stay healthy. Maybe, build a gated community, that cannot be forced into."

"Then, we have to go as far north as possible. The cooler climate, will slow the virus' attack." Jon knew the place had to be far away from large cities and larger populations. The undead, still existed there. They needed seclusion.

As they passed through town after town, the situation seemed the same. They stopped from time to time, to get gas and supplies. Most every place was the same, so much resembling a ghost town. They never saw people, but they suspected the undead.

In a couple of places, Ellie swore she saw the curtains of houses move, when they got out to look around. She felt that feeling, you get when you know you are being watched. She could never prove it though; it was too dangerous to go up to a door and investigate. Still, she wondered if the ones behind the curtains, were human and scared to come outside to see anyone.

In one place, on the southern part of Ohio, they passed through a small town, that reminded them of old TV shows. Where people still had a local pharmacy and local department stores. Ellie insisted they stop. She wanted for a moment, to enjoy the fresh air of the old place.

As they parked, Jon scanned the area. There seemed to be no one there. No one living that is. The streets, still looked like a makeshift graveyard. Just no one was buried. The bodies laid where they died, as the virus or whatever took them.

Ellie looked around at the dead. She wondered who they had been, and what kind of lives they had. She had not gotten used to the remains all around her. She did realize wherever they settled, the dead would have to be cleared, if for no other reason, than to stay healthy. The dead bodies were toxic to the living.

Jon walked ahead of the others, and looked for any sign of life. They were not about to fall into another trap. The children ran behind him, as they saw the local park, which was equipped with a carousel. They begged Jon to take them there, but he worried about the bodies that were surrounding the park.

He took their hands and led them into the park area. The inside seemed to be clean, like no one had used it since the bombings. The kids ran around and looked for their favorite horse, as Jon investigated the controls.

As he reached to the control panel, he flipped the switch that lit the whole carousel up. Then with a couple of buttons pushed, the children felt the horses begin to move and the music came to life. Ellie heard the sound, and looked over at the lights and the children's laughter. She picked up the cat, and moved towards them.

As the carousel spun around, the sounds of life returned to the place of death. It was if it was waiting for them to come save it. Jon watched, as the children acted more normal, than he had ever seen. He smiled, knowing they had escaped the zombie state, they had resorted to so many times.

As Ellie stood watching the lights spinning around, she lost herself in the excitement. Hope hung there, draped over Ellie's shoulder, looking around the town. Everything was fine, until the cat let out a startling hiss, and squirmed into Ellie's arms.

As she turned to see wat was happening, Ellie let out a scream. They had not seen the crown of onlookers, who gathered together in the street. They came from all directions, becoming one on the road behind where Ellie stood.

Jon heard her scream over the loud music, and turned to see the crowd coming for her. He quickly hit the stop button, and powered down the carousel.

Grabbing the children in his arms, he raced towards Ellie. He arrived just as the crowd grew close.

"Jon, they are everywhere." Ellie screamed.

"I know, just run for it." He said, throwing David over his shoulder, and using his free hand to hold tight to Erika.

As they reached the vehicle, the crowd closed in, and Jon hit the gas. He could feel their hands pushing the vehicle back and forth, as he plowed through them to escape. Looking back, Jon saw the crowd turn, and look at them. They moved slowly like controlled automatons. They were not like the undead, but not human either. Jon feared there was a new group of people to stay out of reach of.

Mullins

Chapter Twenty-Two ☢ Into The North

"Ok, is anyone going to speak after that?" Ellie said, as her frustration grew.

Jon had been driving as fast as he could, for over an hour. He did not want to admit, that they let their guard down. He knew better, and after all they had been through and with being captured, he knew better. He just couldn't bring himself to talk about it, until forced to.

"Ok, I screwed up. I let myself get caught off guard…again. I just wanted to let loose for a minute. Now, look where that got us. Surrounded by zombie people. Is this, what life has become?" Jon vented everything he was holding back.

"Well ok then, you had that bottled up. It is good to let it out." Ellie took it all in, as she turned to look at the kids.

In the back seat, the children stared, but not like before. This time, it was in amazement, of Jon's emotional outburst. Ellie knew that look, and she laughed. For all they had been through, it was good to see some humor in it all.

"So, have you thought about a destination?" Ellie asked timidly, as not to set Jon off again.

"Yes, I have thought about this a lot. We need some place that is not heavily populated, and the climate is good for controlling the virus. One place keeps coming to mind…Montana. The mountains are a perfect setting temperature wise, and we should be able to avoid overpopulated areas." Jon finished speaking and looked towards Ellie. "Well?"

"It works. We just have to pick an area, and head for it."

"Already have. As a child, we went to a place called Fort Owen. It is pretty isolated. Originally, it was one of the first pioneer sites in that state. Thing is, it is a day's drive away." He turned to look at her, as if he needed permission.

"Let's do it. What else do we have to do? Stop and be chased by another group of mutants?"

They drove through the night, and into the next day, passing through states and watching the destruction that the war had brought. Ellie was saddened by the death. The life they had, was gone now. There was no normal for her anymore. She looked for the living and found none. Even the birds, were no longer in the trees or the sky.

"I used to love the birds and birdsongs. I don't remember the last time I saw a bird. It's sad we have come to this." Ellie spoke, as she stared out the window.

"Maybe, as we get further into the mountains, we might see animals. We still have a couple of hours to go." Jon tried to comfort her.

"And maybe, we do not have to wait that long." Ellie said, as she pointed through the windshield.

Jon looked out, trying to find a bird, or whatever she had seen. And when he found it, the creature was quite a bit larger. Walking down the middle of the road, was a full-sized grizzly bear.

Jon swerved to miss the bear, as the children sat up in their seat, and watched the large animal fly by. "That, children, was a grizzly bear. That being said, we will need to be on the lookout for wild animals while we live here."

"Hmmm bears…why not, everything else has been after us so far. Why not bears too. I guess they are the most normal thing so far." Ellie broke out into laughter.

As they flew through the mountainous roads, they saw the sign ahead. Just five more miles. The last of their trip flew past, as they pulled up to the entry road. Ellie smiled, as she looked to the opening of the property.

It was surrounded by a wooden fence, that gave it the feel of an old fort. Nothing had changed about this area. It had been spared by the war. The buildings and property were intact.

"This place looks like it was closed up before the war, and no one ever came back to it. No dead bodies to get rid of." Jon observed, as he looked over the area.

"Good, I didn't feel like burning bodies today." Ellie said, with a disgusted look on her face. "What are the chances this place is locked up?

"We will find a way in. We have to get things ready."

"Ready?" Ellie asked.

"When everything is prepared, we send out the signal to all the survivors. We turn this into a homestead for the living." Jon said, as he waved his hand towards the open land, that surrounded the fort.

Chapter Twenty-Three ☢ Lighting The Beacon

Jon walked over to the front doors of the visitor's center. He pushed on the door, hoping it was unlocked. He was mistaken. He looked around, and tried to think of any way inside. There were two other doors on the main level, both were locked as well. Then he looked upwards to the top floor, where a window was opened slightly.

Jon studied the building and the options of getting a person to that level. He looked to Ellie, who had always been a tomboy, but he realized she was not healed enough to take on this task. He ran it through his mind, and looked around, until he realized he could get to the second level by way of the roof.

Climbing up, he made his way over the back slope of the roof, and hung down, until he could step onto the ledge, by the window. As he looked to the ground, he remembered his fear of heights. He shut it out of his mind, as he swung his body around, reached for the open window, and pulled it upwards. With a quick swing, he had his body inside, before falling to the floor.

On the ground, Ellie looked on in fear. What Jon had done was dangerous. He could have killed himself. He was never this risk taking before, he was a timid man when she married him. She figured the war had changed him. The threat of death around every corner was enough to change anyone.

Inside the building, Jon looked around the room he landed in. It was like a bedroom, with more than one bed in it. A sort of group space, for those who worked there, he guessed. As he moved from room to room, there were others just like the first. As he ventured further, he entered one room that was like a huge cafeteria. He wondered why such a place existed in a state park.

As he left the top level, he looked around the lower rooms, to make sure they were really alone. There was no sign of life, just the closed space where a visitor's center once was, as well as offices, and bathrooms. Jon made his way to the back of the visitor office desk, and started opening drawers. If there were keys there, this was where they should be, and his hunch paid off.

Keys in hand, he made his way to the front door, and opened it for the others to come inside. To the kids, this was a magical place, filled with souvenirs and stuffed animals. In reality, it was to be a new home for the foreseeable future.

As Ellie looked around, she was happy with the surroundings. Anything to her, was better than the vehicle. She walked up to Jon and took his hand, as she looked around. Then he led her to the side hall, and pointed to the vending machines. To her surprise, they were stocked with candy and drinks. She was in heaven, and wasted no time heading towards them.

"So, tell me, other than safety, why did you choose this place." Ellie asked him, as she opened the wrapper on a candy bar.

"Because of the safety, there is no fallout here, no undead or zombie types, and we can bring the living toward us." Jon said, proud of his plans.

"And how do we bring people here? We are isolated, and how would they even know we were here in the first place?" Ellie tried to be sympathetic to his plans, but it made no sense to her.

Jon then took her hand, and they walked out the open front door. Ellie followed his lead, as he pulled her forward. When they were clear of the building, he took her to a high grassy peak, as the children trailed behind.

"That is the answer." He said, pointing at a large structure, in the tree line.

"What? You mean the cell tower? What good is that to us? We can call on the cell, but who will answer?" Ellie said sarcastically.

"Nope, not a cell tower. It is a direct satellite link up. Anything we send here, can go anywhere a satellite can receive the signal."

"And all the satellites, are still in orbit, since the nukes were at ground level, and on the moon. We can still access them." Ellie said excitedly. Wow, you are pretty smart sometimes."

"Yeah, I know." He laughed. "But seriously, we can use this, like the Amber Alert system, or when they tell you of impending storms, or severe weather."

"I remember those, back when the phones still worked all the time. I wonder how many people, still have their phones with them?" Ellie asked.

"We do, why wouldn't others. The signal is in and out in all areas, but it does work."

"Yeah, until the grid goes down completely. I mean, if no one is maintaining the power stations, how long will the power last." She said grimly.

"You know the good thing about this place?" Jon asked. "When I was on the roof, it is covered with solar panels. It can support itself."

Ellie smiled at the good fortune they had finally found. She hugged Jon, and turned to look at the children playing in the grass. They had seemed to shrug off being taken hostage. In time, she was sure she could help them be normal all the time. In this new place, they had little to fear.

"When do we start to broadcast a signal?" Ellie asked.

"As soon as we decide what to send. We probably do not want to initially disclose where we are, until we can make sure who answers back. Being cautious is the key. I think out initial signal should be one asking if anyone is still alive out there."

Jon and Ellie moved into their new home, and investigated everything there was to find about the place. Inside the tower, they found it to be fully operational, with its own solar panels to power it in case of emergency. They traced the controls back to the main building of the park.

As they gathered around, Jon studied the controls. It all seemed straight forward, and what he did not know, he read the manuals to find out. After hours of preparing, he turned to Ellie, and got ready to fire up the system.

As the computer came online, Jon stared at the screen. It all made sense to him, as he made his way through the menus. He typed his initial message in. His words were simply, 'Seeking survivors of the war. If you are out there, respond by text. We have found safety, in a place in the north."

Jon turned to Ellie. "If there is anyone out there who gets this, then maybe they will reply.

"There has to be others, who have made it. We four, are not the only ones on earth." Ellie was hopeful.

As they turned to walk away, neither had hope for an instant reply. Just as they reached the doorway, the pinging noise began. One by one, the texts clicked through the computer screen. Texts from all around the world, flooded the list.

Ellie turned to Jon and smiled. "I don't think we are alone anymore."

"Now the real journey begins." John replied.

Concept Art

Mullins

Armageddon

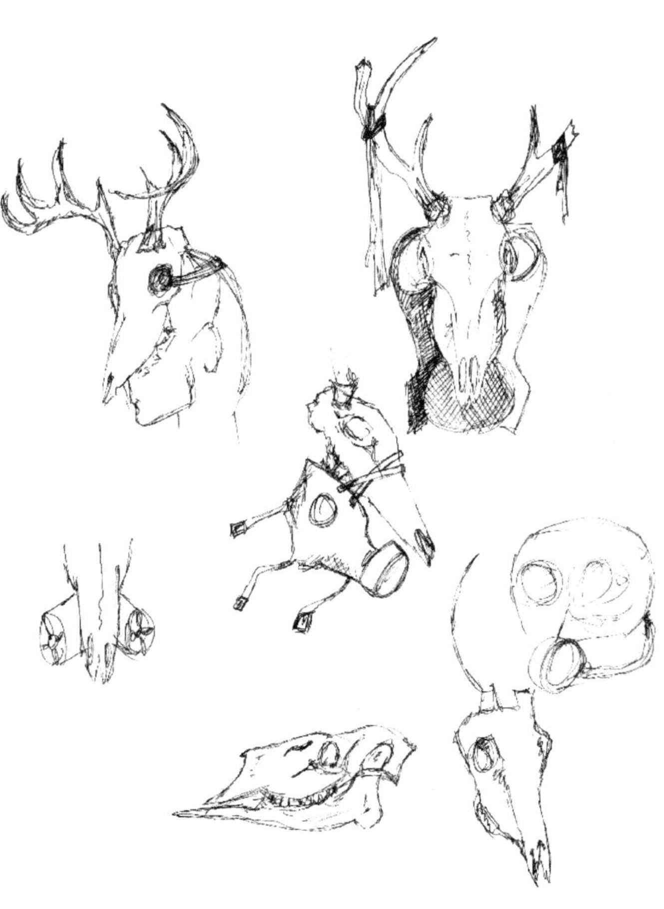

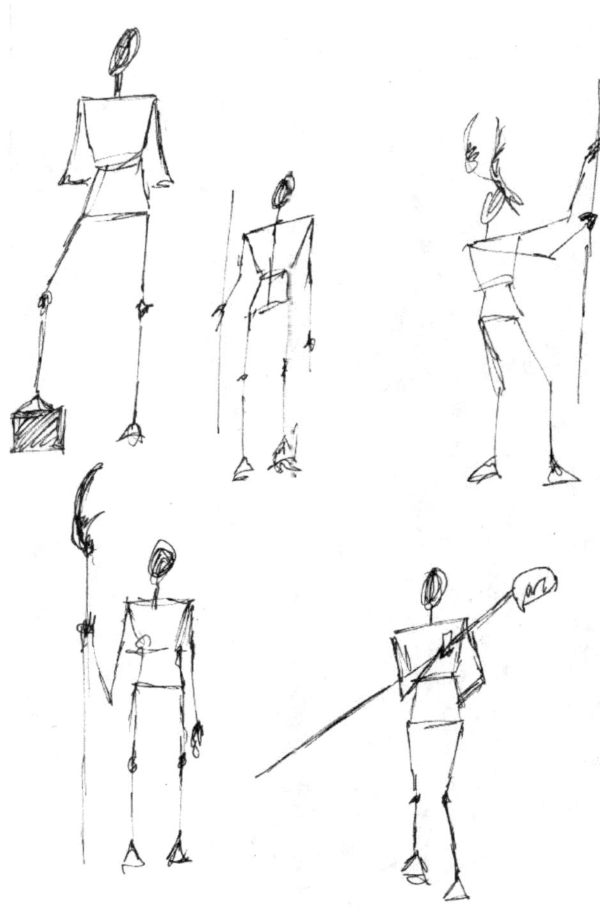

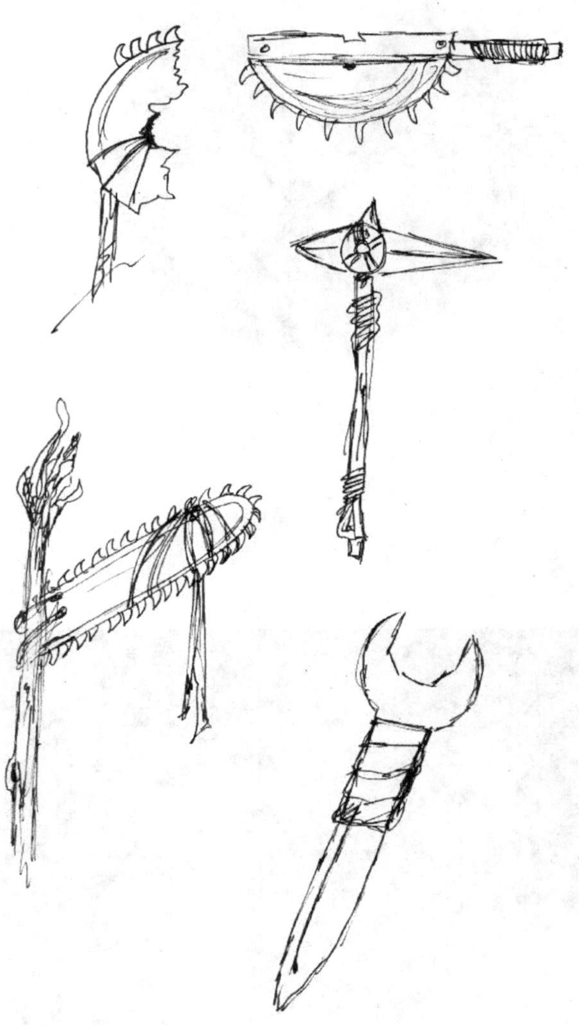

ARMAGEDDON

Included next are the first chapters of G.W. Mullins' Best-Selling title

**Rise of The DarkLighter Book One
Dark Awakening**

From the Author of the Best-Selling
Book Series "From The Dead Of Night"

Rise of the Darklighter

Book One

Dark Awakening

To fight evil, you
have to embrace
the darkness.

G.W. Mullins

Rise Of The Dark-Lighter Book One

Dark Awakening

Is Available in Hardback (978-1-64871-256-2),

Paperback (978-1-64871-159-6) and various eBook

formats worldwide.

Nuestra Señora de la Santa Muerte, also known as Santa Muerte, is an idol, female deity or folk saint in Mexican and Mexican-American Catholicism. The personification of death, she is believed to be associated with healing, protection, and delivering her devotees safely into the afterlife. Many consider her an angel of death.

Mullins

Before

The lightning struck around them, as Malachi struggled to steer the car through the debris that the storm threw in their way. His heart raced and he could feel the pounding in his chest. He was scared, probably more scared than he had ever been before. For once in his self-absorbed life, this was not about him, a life was on the line.

"Hang on Uncle, I am doing my best to get us to the hospital. The storm is not making this easy." Malachi tried to comfort him.

"I know, I am holding on. You know I never said how proud I am of you." Carl's voice trailed off into a cough.

"Be still Uncle. There will be time for that after I get you to the hospital."

As Malachi spoke, he attempted to wipe the condensation from the windshield of the car. His efforts were in vain, as he would finish wiping, the fogginess would return. The car was old and barely drivable, it should not have been on the road, but in this situation, he had no choice.

As Malachi looked away to slap his hand against the defroster, he took his eyes off the road. It was then the storm took its vengeance and a funnel cloud passed in front of them. As its winds ripped through the road, a huge oak tree began to sway. Malachi looked up just in time to see it uprooted and flying towards the car.

Malachi let out a scream, as he knew there was nothing he could do to get out of the tree's path. As the tree hit the front grill of the car, it spun out of control and rolled down the deserted street. Flipping end over end, the crushed vehicle landed at the white picket fence that surrounded a country church.

As he looked out through the broken windshield, Malachi felt the blood running down his forehead. Struggling to lift his arm to his head, he felt the pain of being thrown around the vehicle in the crash. He was not sure, but the pain in his chest felt like a cracked rib. The pain came in jabs with his every movement. At first, he did not think of his uncle, then the realization hit him, he was not hearing any noise from the back seat.

Malachi turned to look around. A feeling of dread washed over him. How could his uncle have survived? The man was at death's door before the crash. Looking to the backseat, there was nothing. He was alone in the car.

Looking up through the broken glass, he scanned the road, until he found the form of a body laying several feet behind. His heart sank as he assumed the worst. He had failed with is most important thing he had ever had to do. Pushing against the seat, Malachi attempted to move his battered body to the driver's side door. He pulled the handle and leaned in, but the door was bent and mangled.

Leaning back, Malachi pulled his legs to his chest. He felt the surge of pain as he tried to hold them back with his arms. With all the energy he could muster, he let loose and kicked the door. It flew open quickly, and with such a force, that it slammed into the fender and then to the ground.

Malachi crawled out of the opening and fell to his knees. His head spun around, as dizziness overtook him. The rain blasted all around, as he tried to look towards his uncle. With every drop that hit his head, the blood that covered him splattered and ran down his face. It was no time, before his entire face was covered in red. His eyes stung and burned as he tried to focus, and began to try to get to his feet.

He wobbled back and forth, and lost his footing, falling to the ground as soon as he stood up. He was determined. His mind raced and his life flashed before him. He had accomplished nothing in the twenty years he had been alive. His past was a blur of selfishness and a desire to acquire money.

As he slammed into the paved road, his parent's faces ran through his mind. He wondered if they would have been ashamed of him. He never considered it before. They died when he was very young. He barely knew them. It was then his uncle Carl came and took him in. Malachi felt tears welling in his burning eyes, as he realized the only person on earth that cared for him, was just a few feet away and dying.

Malachi pushed his hands onto the pavement and forced himself upwards. Crawling at first, he finally got his footing and made his way to the lifeless body he saw before him. He fell to his knees at Carl's side and screamed out.

"Be still young one, I am not dead yet." A quiet shaky voice came from Carl's lips.

"Uncle, you are alive. I thought you were…"

"Dead…you can say the word. We all must die sometime, just not this minute. Perhaps soon though." Carl began to cough with his last words.

"No, I will get you help. I promise you I will."

"Malachi, just calm yourself. Go to the church and see if anyone is there. If the priest is in, get him to come and bring me inside."

Malachi rose to his feet, and moved as quickly as he could, to the church doors. As he pulled at the handles, the doors did not move. They were locked. Malachi knew he had to find a way to get his uncle out of the storm. He drew back his fists and threw them at the red wooden door. He screamed out, as he beat on the wood, and threw himself against it trying to force his way in. Just as he was about to give up, the door opened.

"What is happening here?" Father Timothy said hastily as he looked down and saw the bloody face of Malachi. "What has happened to you my boy?"

"The storm, it caused the car to crash and my uncle is badly hurt."

"Why would you come out in a mess like this anyway?" The priest asked.

"My uncle was ill before we left, I think he is dying. Please, can you help him?"

The two made their way to Carl, who was passing in and out of consciousness. Father Timothy took hold of him, and Malachi assisted as they lifted Carl from the ground. The rain pounded down heavily upon them, as they made their way to the door of the church.

Safely inside, they laid Carl's limp body on a pew, near the front of the chapel. Carl's lips moved as if he was speaking to someone. Malachi was not sure of who, he was not sure he wanted to know. He was only sure he was more scared than he had ever been. He looked down at his hands, as they shook uncontrollably. He tried not to succumb to his fears.

The priest returned with towels and a cup of hot tea. As he reached down to Malachi, the boy just looked up to him, barely able to form words. Taking the drink, Malachi held it in his hands, warming them as the priest began to wipe the blood from his forehead and face. Malachi smiled at him trying to find the strength to say thank-you.

"Your uncle needs help that I cannot provide. I can take care of the spiritual end, but honestly, that will not save him. He needs a doctor and medicine. From the looks of him, he was having a heart attack, long before you came out into the storm." Father Timothy said as he continued to clean Malachi's wounds.

"How do we get a doctor? The storm is worse than before. I cannot go anywhere without a car." The boy said, as he hung his head.

"You cannot go anywhere regardless, you are injured. The storm is no place for you in your condition. I will go. I know the roads, and a few shortcuts."

"But how will you get there? You can't walk in this storm."

"I have a motorcycle. It was donated to the church years ago. and I have become very good at riding it. Don't look at me like that, I might be a priest, but I can do normal things you know. Stay here and watch over your uncle. I will be back as soon as I can."

"Father, please be careful. Oh, and thank-you for what you are about to do."

Timothy acknowledged him, and turned to go. Malachi admired his bravery. He wished he was braver than he was. He returned to his uncle's side looking down at him. Carl was still moving his mouth as if he were speaking. The words were not intelligible, but still he spoke under his breath.

As Malachi watched, his uncle's eyes flew open and he pulled his arms close to his chest. Calling out, his voice began to make sense, and his words were clearer. He looked to Malachi and stretched out an arm to grab at him.

Malachi went down on his knees and took his uncle's hand. "What is it uncle. Are you feeling better?"

"No, my boy, I am fighting. The demons of death are coming for me. I need help to fight them. I need you to pray for me. Pray to Santa Muerte, ask her to help me. She will come."

"Uncle, she is not real, she is only a myth. Old Spanish women prey to her as a way to escape their unhappiness." Malachi insisted.

"She is not a myth, she is real. I have known many who have seen her, she comes when life is about to end. She can save me. Please do this for me. You must give her an offering. Place a bowl of water at the alter and pray to her."

"I do not believe in this or in religion, but if it will calm you, I will do it. Now rest as I go find water."

As Malachi searched through the building, he found the kitchen and a bowl for the water. As he filled it, he shook his head, not believing he was about to participate in this craziness. In his heart he knew he had to do it, if for no other reason, to calm his uncle until help came.

Malachi returned to the chapel and placed the water near a statue and cross, in the front of the room. As he kneeled on the floor, he looked up at the Virgin Mary. He wished he believed, in this religion, or in anything that would help them. His heart was too cold and barren he thought.

As he bowed his head, he began to ask for help from Santa Muerte. He asked her to come to him, to aid him in the saving of his uncle. He offered her the bowl of water as an act of respect. Then he closed his eyes. He called for help, and the darkness answered back.

The light in the room faded, as a shadow came forward from the darkened back wall. The figure of a woman took shape. She had dark features and her head was bowed. As she slowly walked forward, Malachi looked up. He prepared to scream, as she raised a shriveled finger to her dried lips.

As he looked at her, he could make out her face, it was drawn and looked as if she had been dead. She retained the features of a woman, but was as much skeleton as human. Her skin looked as if it had been wrapped around bone with no real meat left to her body. Malachi was scared, and his heart raced as she slowly moved towards him.

As she came in his direction, Malachi fell backwards from the feet of the statue. He scrambled trying to get upright. A scream became trapped in his lips as he crawled to the side of his uncle.

Leaning down, Santa Muerte picked up the bowl of water. She moved it to her leathery looking lips and allowed the water to pass into her mouth. She drank until the water was gone. Then she sat the bowl back down and turned towards them.

Malachi stared at her, as she began to smile. As he looked, her appearance began to change. With every second, she became more human in appearance. Her skeletal structure became more flesh-like. Her body filled out, and her face became normal. She laughed out-loud as the transformation became complete.

"Your offering is accepted. I needed that. But why have you disturbed my sleep. It has been many years since I graced this plane. No one has called out to me in over a decade." Santa Muerte looked at him inquisitively.

"My uncle, he is ill. I fear he is dying. Please save him." Malachi pleaded with her.

Extending a hand, she reached down and touched Carl's head. She smiled at him as Carl looked back to her. A joy rushed over him as he saw that Malachi had done as he asked. Carl sat up as Santa Muerte cradled him in her arms.

"Your time to leave this plane was not meant to be as of yet." She spoke softly.

"What do you mean? Is he not dying?"

"That is not what I meant. He was not supposed to die for some time yet. His fate has changed."

"Can you save him?" Malachi pleaded for answers.

"It does not work that way ignorant boy. Life cannot just be given. It is an exchange. A life for a life. One forfeits, so another may live. For him to continue in this existence, another must take his place in death. Now that wouldn't be fair, would it boy?" She asked him.

"No, but I do not want him to die. You have to save him."

"Not everything is by your human choosing. If he is to live, then you tell me whose life to claim in his place. Would you choose that I take the life of the priest that left here unselfishly trying to save another, or perhaps another innocent who does not even know you. Or perhaps, you are willing to exchange your life for his?" She laughed out hysterically, as she walked around looking at the statues in the church.

"No, this cannot be. Malachi, do not even consider her offer. If this is the only way, then I choose death. Take me now Angel of Death. I believed in you and what you stand for. I had no idea you were so cruel and heartless." Carl screamed at her.

"Heartless," she laughed. "I am here to save you, and you call me heartless. I should strike you down myself for your disrespect. I was human like you, and I know the pain of death. You lived much longer than I did. Do not whine to me about your pathetic life. If you want to live, a choice must be made."

"Is there no other way?" Malachi pleaded with her.

"Perhaps, there is. I tire of coming here to this existence to take lives. Become my apprentice, help in my work. Then in the time of one year, you can win back your freedom, if you fulfill your duties."

"You mean, I would not die, and I can come back to my life."

"As pathetic as it is. Yes, you can return, but only at a time I agree. Your Uncle will live, and may do so until his actual time of death that was ordained."

"Then I agree to your terms." Malachi choked on his words.

"No, Malachi do not let her take you. She will not honor the deal. Run from here." Carl screamed.

"It is too late old man, I have him now. The deal is struck. He is mine."

As she turned to look back at Carl, she reached out a hand and Malachi took it. As they walked towards the back hall of the church, they both faded into darkness. Carl stood up, feeling the energy flowing through him again. He was healed, and his life returned. Malachi was not so lucky.

Chapter 1 - Out of The Past

Santa Muerte stood looking, through her portal into the past. She thought about her new apprentice. She watched as he slept. Her mind raced to when she was still human. Moving her hand over the portal, she saw the mist change within, the images went back to the time of 1847. The Mexican-American war raged through Texas. She stared on until she saw herself.

She clung to her mother, as they made their way through the side street trying to avoid the spray of bullets. Her mother pulled her close. Fear covered her face; she had no idea how to save them. They were surrounded by the fighting.

As her mother pulled her into the shelter at the end of the house, Anna looked up to her. She did not understand what was happening. Her mother clung to her trying to quiet her cries.

"Anna…" Her mother spoke. Santa Muerte played the moment over and over again. It had been so long since she had heard her own name said, or her mother's voice saying it. Her cold heart throbbed in her chest. She wasn't supposed to feel this way anymore. She had given up feeling anything about life or people years ago. It was too much of a toll on her. When she inherited her role as an angel of death, she left so much behind.

Looking back into the past, she watched her mother as she cared for Anna who was only six. This war was no place for her. Children were supposed to be carefree and happy. She should have been playing somewhere in a field of flowers. Instead, she was facing an army of soldiers. Santa Muerte glanced down for a moment, she knew what was coming, and that much could still hurt her.

"Mi amor, I promise this is not what I planned for you in life. Please, no matter what happens, remember mama loved you so much. If I could have changed this, I would have. I just do not know how to save you or myself."

As Carlotta finished speaking, she heard the soldiers making their way down the side street. She pulled Anna close and covered her mouth. "Do not cry, do not make a sound." She whispered, as the door began to open slowly. Carlotta raised her head as she came eye to eye with the enemy she had come to fear.

"Stand up woman." He screamed at her.

"Please, I beg of you, spare my child." She cried out.

As the soldier studied her, he did not care for her or her child. He raised his rifle into the air. A smile crossed his lips, as he prepared to claim another notch for his collection of kills. The shot rang out, as Anna watched her mother fall sideways on the ground.

Anna screamed and grabbed at her mother. She pulled at Carlotta's hand, but she did not move.

Anna struggled to arouse her mother, it was no use, she was gone. The young girl had no concept of death or murder. In that day, she witnessed both within minutes. She stood looking at her mother and screaming, as the soldier reloaded his rifle.

"Looks like my lucky day, two Mexicans at the same time. Don't worry, it will be over soon." He said laughing at Anna.

She stood there watching, paralyzed by her own fear. Santa Muerte yelled at her, "Why don't you run and hide. Just save yourself." She raised her hands to her head, as the sound of the rifle firing, rang through the room. Clutching her chest, she caressed the point where the bullet had hit her. If she still had a heart, she thought it would hurt.

Her eyes filled with tears as she watched. The soldier left, walking away proud of himself and his deeds. She felt hatred filling her. She grinned, and thought to herself, there must still be some emotions left inside somewhere. As the killer turned to leave the alley, a Mexican soldier came from around the corner and fired before he was seen. The murderer fell to the ground, a grim look on his face. As he looked up, he saw the dark one coming for him.

A few feet away, the dark shadow came. As it moved forward, it took shape. A man emerged from within the darkness. Dressed in black from head to toe, he wore a dress suit and looked like an undertaker. Looking about, the dark one studied the area. "So many dead, so many souls to claim. I'll be here a while." The Angel of Death was pleased.

He cleared the street of the dead before surveying the area. He made his way down the street until finding the bodies of Carlotta and Anna. Looking down at Anna, he shook his head. "Little One, you never had a chance in life, did you?"

As he lifted Anna into his arms, he carried her through the streets. His pain was obvious, as he struck out at those who caused the death of such a young girl. In moments, he killed all who were in the immediate area, before lifting himself upwards with the child still in his arms.

In his own realm, he took Anna to his private chamber. There he took a small amount of his power and formed a ball of energy in front of him. Looking down at the girl, he aimed his hand, shooting the power within her. "My child, forgive me for what I do, but this is the only way I know to give you life again." With the power surging through her, she took a deep breath, and sat up coughing.

"Arise Muerte. My child, born of death."

"My name is Anna, she said staring at him."

"You were Anna, now you are so much more. You are Queen of the Dead."

"I don't understand." She questioned him.

"In time, it will all make sense to you. But for now, you will grow and learn."

As his words echoed through the room, Malachi watched from behind. He had been watching the whole time. He understood a little

better what was happening. He had enlisted his soul
with that of the dead.

In order to save his uncle, Malachi is forced to summon Santa Muerte, the deity of death. With his soul on the line, he must do her bidding, to regain his freedom.

To fight evil, you have to embrace the darkness

Rise Of The DarkLighter

From Best-Selling Author

G.W. Mullins

Dark Awakening
Night Of The Demon
Available in Hardback, Paperback and eBook

Daniel walked in the land of the dead. Now the dead want him back!
For Information About
From The Dead
Of Night
The Book Series Visit
gwmullins.wixsite.com/books

About the Author

Thanks for choosing this book, if you enjoyed it, please leave positive feedback.

G.W. Mullins is an Author, Photographer, and Entrepreneur of Native American / Cherokee descent. He has been a published author for over 13 years. His writing has focused on the paranormal and Native American studies.

Mullins has released several books on the history/stories/fables of the Native American Indians. Among his books are the extremely successful "Star People, Sky Gods and Other Tales of the Native American Indians," "Story Teller An Anthology Of Folklore From The Native American Indians," "The Native American Story Book - Stories Of The American Indians For Children Volumes 1-5," "The Native American Cookbook," and "Walking With Spirits Native American Myths, Legends, And Folklore Volumes 1 Thru 6."

He has released the complete series of his Sci/fi Fantasy books "From The Dead Of Night," including the Best-Selling titles – "Daniel Is Waiting" and

"Daniel Returns." His most recent work includes the series "Rise Of The Snow Queen" featuring Book One "The Polar Bear King", Book Two "War Of The Witches", and Book Three "The Story of Gerda And Kai."

Mullins' latest releases include two young adult fantasy series, "Rise of the Darklighter" Book One "Dark Awakening," Book Two "Night Of The Demon" and the "Dream Walker" Book Series featuring "Enter the Sandman" and "Wide Awake In Dream Land." Among his other releases are "The Legend Of White Bear (Extended edition)" a Native American paranormal shapeshifting story, "Messages from The Other Side" (a nonfiction book about communication with the dead), and the currently releasing "The Convergence" (a post-apocalyptic book multi-series event).

For further information, on his writing, visit G.W. Mullins' web site at ***http://gwmullins.wix.com/books***.

<u>Also Available From G.W. Mullins</u>

The Convergence Book Zero Mass Destruction

Rise of the Darklighter Book One Dark Awakening

Rise of the Darklighter Book Two Night Of The Demon

Rise Of The Snow Queen Book Three The Story Of Gerda And Kai

Rise Of The Snow Queen Book Two The War Of The Witches

Rise Of The Snow Queen Book One The Polar Bear King

Daniel Awakens A Ghost Story Begins– From The Dead Of Night Prequel

Daniel Is Waiting A Ghost Story – From The Dead Of Night Book One

Daniel Returns A Ghost Story - From The Dead Of Night Book Two

Armageddon

Daniel's Fate A Ghost Story Ends - From The Dead
Of Night Book Four

Dream Walker Book Two Wide Awake In Dream
Land

Dream Walker Book One Enter The Sand Man

Nick Grainger Book One The Curse Of Cleopatra

The Legend Of White Bear (Extended Edition)

Messages From The Other Side Stories of the Dead,
Their Communication, and Unfinished Business

Vengeance – A Paranormal Mystery

Mysteries Of The Unseen World – Ghost, Hauntings
and The Unexplained

Haunted America Stories Of Ghost, Hauntings And
The Unexplained

Timeless – A Paranormal Romance Murder Mystery

Star People, Sky Gods, And Other Tales Of The
Native American Indians

Mullins

More Star People, Sky Gods, And Other Paranormal
Tales Of The Native American Indians

Lost Tales Of The Native American Indians Vol 1

Walking With Spirits Native American Myths,
Legends, And Folklore Volumes One Thru Six

The Native American Cookbook

Native American Cooking - An Indian Cookbook
With Legends And Folklore

The Native American Story Book - Stories Of The
American Indians For Children
Volumes One Thru Five

The Best Native American Stories For Children

Cherokee A Collection of American Indian Legends,
Stories And Fables

Creation Myths - Tales Of The Native American
Indians

Strange Tales Of The Native American Indians

Armageddon

Spirit Quest - Stories Of The Native American
Indians

Animal Tales Of The Native American Indians

Medicine Man - Shamanism, Natural Healing,
Remedies And Stories Of The Native American
Indians

Native American Legends: Stories Of The Hopi
Indians Volumes One and Two

Totem Animals Of The Native Americans

The Best Native American Myths, Legends And
Folklore Volumes One Thru Three

Ghosts, Spirits And The Afterlife In Native American
Indian Mythology And Folklore

War Song: Tales Of The Native American Indians

Origin Tales Of The Native American

For books available from G.W. Mullins in Hardback,
Paperback and eBook

Visit: https://gwmullins.wixsite.com/books

Or scan the QR Code below

Links to G.W. Mullins pages are on Linktree
https://linktr.ee/gw.mullins